FITTICK
Fisher of Men

AN IMAGINED BIOGRAPHY OF ST FITTICK, 7TH CENTURY AD

WHO LIVED AND WORKED ON THE BAY OF NIGG, TORRY

Beatrice Hale

First published in 2022 by The Kellas Cat Press, Aberdeen.

ISBN: 978-1-910926-84-0

Cover illustration by Sheila Donald

DEDICATION

TO MY DEAR FRIENDS COLIN AND JEANETTE GIBSON,

WHOSE GIFT OF A BEAUTIFUL VASE

WITH THE PAINTING OF AN IMAGINARY FITTICK

INSPIRED THIS STORY.

And thank you to my kind family, who listen patiently.

INTRODUCTION

This tale is inspired by the story of the Irish monk Fittick being washed up on the shores of Nigg Bay, perhaps in 630 AD or thereabouts. A Well sprang up as he touched ground on the shores of Nigg Bay. When I was a child I loved to imagine what he might have done, in our special place where we went to picnic and play. This was Fittick-land, where he lived and worked long ago. So what did he do? What could he have done? We used to wonder.

Fittick, originally from Ireland, or possibly the son of the King of Dalriada, is an enigma. He is a man of many names, Fittick, Mofotacus, Fiacre and others. According to different sources, it seems that he lived between the years of 600 and 670 AD, and was in some way subject to the Bishop of Meaux in Paris. It seems, too, that when he was an Irish monk preaching the gospel in France he had a vision. In this vision he was ordered to get to the coast and take the first ship bound for the north. But how his journey was inaugurated, whether through a vision, or by missionary zeal or order of a bishop, Fittick certainly sailed to bring the gospel to Scotland.

His exact destination is not known. How he came to be in Nigg is also not known. One suggestion is that the ship's crew were superstitious about having a priest on board and took the chance of a very stormy day in the waters off north-east Scotland to push him overboard. He thus landed on the shores of the Bay of Nigg. Other stories have it that he was washed from the boat during a huge storm.

His activities there are obscure. He might have penetrated into Aberdeen itself, but there seems to be no evidence for such a move. After some years, presumably in north-east Scotland, he then may have returned to France. One story is that he performed a miracle of clearing a forest by a wave of his hand. He became the patron saint of gardeners, and he is also known as St Fiacre, and the patron saint of taxi drivers. Various sources have provided this information, and there is very little more.

He has always been present in many lives. All my family belonged to and attended St Fittick's Church in Walker Road, Torry. After church attendance in summer, I remember being taken on family picnics to the shores of the Bay of Nigg. Later, as an adult, I explored the old churchyard where my great grandmother, Mary Robertson, is buried. I wandered round the walls of the ruined kirk, imagining what Fittick (or Mofotacus or Fiacre) did on the shores of Nigg, once he landed there.

We do know that he lived in the Bay of Nigg. On the shore there was the Blessed Well of Unspoken Water, said to have risen up as his hand touched the ground when he landed from the boat. Slightly up the hill, there are the remains of the old Church, dating back to the late 1600s or early 1700s, with its ancient churchyard and burials up to early 20th century times. Recent excavations have shown that this church, rebuilt two or three times, retains its important 'leper's squint' window, where those from the nearest leprosarium in Tullos could participate in the service, without entering the church itself, and thus not meeting with the congregation.

In this story I have returned to my roots, where St Fittick shared much of my life. I have imagined his thoughts, words and feelings, and have created a series of scenarios whereby Fittick brought Christianity into the north-east of Scotland. Based on some knowledge of the missionary work of Columba and Colman of Portmahomack, I have pictured him in the Bay of Nigg and the outskirts of Torry, moving amongst the settlements there, preaching, teaching, interacting – and performing miracles.

This book is an imagined biography of a much-loved figure in my childhood and while I have taken some liberties with the past and the environment, I decided this was acceptable in the construction of the story. So enjoy the meanderings of an interested Torry quine who has decided to envisage how her favourite saint took the Good News to her home country, and how he lived there.

CHAPTER ONE

At last on the move! His dream was about to happen. April, and reckoning the six hundred and thirtieth year after the birth of our Saviour. Six centuries after Christ, and he, Fittick, to be His missioner, to work for Him, teach His words and show Him to the world. Fittick stretched his arms to embrace this world. His dark hair ruffled in the breeze, grey eyes gazing into the distance, and even beyond, into other worlds, other times. His mission was about to begin. Here and now!

The rays of the warm sun glanced over the small waves of the river Seine, making them sparkle as the oars splashed gently down on the water, and as it dripped from the blades, the rhythm of the oars pushing the boat along. This small boat was to take him to the mouth of the Seine. Then he would climb on to a bigger fishing boat, and sail north, past other kingdoms, to the land of the Scots. Some monks had already begun the task of bringing the gospel to these people. There were the renowned Ninian, Columba in Iona, and Machar in Aberdeen, and there was Columbanus in Portmahomack. But there was much, much more to be done.

Even the journey would not be easy. He knew, of course, the story of Jonah, and had heard that even yet many fishermen still believed strongly in witchcraft and the evil eye, and that they needed at times to turn away men of religion. And then life as a missionary to these unbelievers would not be easy. But the Bishop had said there were already some converts, and people working for Christ and God. The land of the Scots was to be his destination, and this was to be his learning of how to minister and preach. Fittick was grateful that his first ministry was to be with some of his own kind (for the Scots and the Irish had much in common), where he could learn, confer and find support.

The small boat pushed into the jetty at the curve of the Seine as it flowed into the ocean. Fittick moved on shore, grabbing at his belongings. Never could he go anywhere without his Gospels, nor his beautiful crucifix. His mother had given them to him, so he prized them even more than their support for his calling.

He walked round the small harbour, stretching and enjoying flat steady land, before boarding the bigger fishing boat for the longer stretch.

It was much larger than the small rowing boat he'd taken from the Bishop's Palace to be carried down river. This boat was ready for the deep sea and big catches. The deck was curved, wider in the centre, narrowing towards the stern and to the bow, where the nets were held. There was space for seating for the rowers, and for the fishermen dropping nets over the side. There was also a small space for cooking, for the journeys to the fishing areas were long and slow.

Though the seas were fairly calm, he still suffered from seasickness, and struggled to keep his balance on the curving deck. He could see heads shaking and surreptitious smiles which gave him an idea of the general thinking. Clearly the comments were of the ilk, 'Not a fisherman, no!' and 'No sailor this one!' And others looked at him furtively, sideways, with sidelong glances. He wasn't sure if he was meant to observe such stealthy glares, nor did he let himself flinch at the occasional thump in the ribs, or the most meagre portions of food.

He perched, shivering, in the place he had been given on the deck, out of the way of the hard work. He was lucky to have this, he thought as he eased himself into the narrow space. As well as the pushes and shoves, and the minimal food, his small space was messy. It was sea-weed dirty, smelly and, scrunched into the corner was a thin, torn, grubby, blanket. He pulled it over his shivering legs and looked round, face screwed up with seasickness. Groaning, he muttered. 'Why? why me? What am I doing here? Oh, God! Help!'

A couple of the seamen laughed at him.

'We need prayers! You can pray for good winds.'

Two or three others looked hostile. Only one or two were friendly. He needed to be careful who he talked with and sat with, and what he said. A hard lesson for a keen new priest, he thought, huddled into his smelly clothes, clutching the boatrail to keep his balance.

The morning wind blustered round the sails, the sea was rough, the boat heaved up and down. But, he told himself, Christ, the Son of God, had suffered greatly and given His life. Who was he, Fittick, to complain about *his* life? Straining his eyes through the splashing of the waves, he hoped to catch a glimpse of passing land. And squirming further along the narrow boat, he found a small space on the boards where, if he settled down, he could keep a steady lookout. He clung to the railing to avoid being thrown from side to side. Even so he was still battered and jolted. The fishermen grinned at his struggles. They were more experienced, more sure-footed, and better balanced. Some held out a helping hand. But some hands were used to push the young priest even further off balance.

The boat was ploughing on through waves which seemed to be getting higher and higher. Fittick had to strain his head backwards to see the wave tops and hopefully, a bit of sky.

Whoosh! One wave came soaring over the boat. Everyone was soaked. The boat dipped and rose again. And again. And another wave surged and crashed on to the deck, sliding over the boat. He was soaked to the skin, hair clinging to his scalp, dribbling on to his shoulders, tunic drenched and dripping. And he was terrified. Child-like prayers whispered from his lips.

'Please God, make it stop. Please God, help!'

The boat steadied, he thought, and he opened his eyes. Did he see land way beyond the boat? He blinked and pointed.

One of the crew nodded to Fittick.

'Over there, there's the land of the Scots. That's a north bay, near the village of Torry. And we're near our own fishing grounds at last.'

Fittick nodded. It meant little to him, but he supposed that the boat would heave-to as the nets were dropped over the side. And maybe there would be a little more steadiness with the nets trawling along, and becoming laden with fish. Perhaps he could land, and make his way north on foot? Or was the boat really destined for the coast of Scotland? He had been told so, but with the fierce storms, he wondered whether a journey by land would easier.

WHOOSH! This time the wave was higher than a cliff, as blue and black as the bruises on his forearm, and as white at the top as his grandmother's fringe of hair. He dared not move from his place lest the slippery deck slide him down and off the boat. He tried to shield himself from the wave's crashing descent. All he could do was to hang on to the boat rail with both hands, head down, chin tucked into cape and tunic, the knotted prayer rope round his waist trailing down to his knees.

The wave came thundering down. Fittick was covered with such a flow of water that his hands were wrenched from their tight hold, and his body was lifted off the deck in a surge of movement. He reached out for help but there was no helping hand nearby. Rather, he felt a push on his back, sending him forwards. And he lost consciousness. His body slamming down stirred his senses again and he felt beneath him for the planks of the deck.

But there was no deck. There was nothing but water! Nothing firm beneath him. No deck. Only water. Wet, cold, rough, and soft – no strength, no platform beneath him, only the yielding waters ready to receive his body. He was sinking. Down, far down, into the icy depths. His confusion was such that, for a short time, he let himself sink.

Then furiously he struck out for the surface. He wanted - he *needed* to stay on top. That way the fishermen would see him, and rescue him, he hoped. His hand caught a short, broken plank of wood. And another. One for each hand. At least these would help him stay on top, help him float, he thought.

But … what if they came from the boat itself? What if … the thought was horrible … the boat had split?

He raised his head, shaking the water from his eyes, ducking as the waves caught him again. But he had seen no boat. No wreckage. No other men.

What had happened? He continued to kick frantically, and to clutch the broken bits of wood to help him stay on the surface.

The wind was howling. The tide was moving fast. He could feel himself being waved towards some dark mass maybe of trees, maybe of a hillside. The waves thundered him along. He tried to cry out, but his feeble shout could never have been heard above the noise of the storm. The waves pushed again. And again, and again, with his breath being forced from his body, his arms and legs waving to try to direct himself towards the dark mass of land. He spewed water, he pushed his face up, his arms and legs worked and kicked, until at last, he found himself smacked down on to a sandy patch, with pebbles beneath his body. The wave left him there and its movement back into the ocean made a huge noise on the shingle.

He shook his head and water flew from him, his mouth, nose and ears. His hair was dripping wet, his clothes saturated. He dug his fingers into the shingle, feeling its grittiness as a welcome contrast to the waves. He gasped and gasped again, trying desperately to get a decent flow of air and breath in his mouth.

A shout came from above him, competing with the wind.

'Look! Look! Nearly drookit.'

He didn't understand the words. But he did understand when a tall man knelt by him, felt his head and his arms and legs, and turned him over on to his back.

'What happened to you?'

Fittick shook his head. He was too far gone to speak in any tongue, Irish or Scots Gaelic, or even Latin and French. He felt himself being lifted and carried along. Well, if he was a prisoner, so be it. He could only wait and see.

But he was in the land of the Scots!

CHAPTER TWO

Two men carried him from the water's edge up the shingle towards the grassy edge of the hill. Sea water was dripping from his clothes, his prayer rope trailed beneath him. He felt sick, turned his head down to vomit, and the spew went over the rough leggings of his porter. Fittick groaned in disgust and fear.

'Never mind, never mind. It'll wash.'

One of the rescuers spoke above his head. He was a cheery soul and the words struck a lighter note but Fittick felt too ill to respond. Nor did he understand the words, only the tone. He groaned again and retched. The carriers stopped, put him down and waited while he vomited.

It lasted only a few minutes, and then he sat up. One of his rescuers handed him a lump of moss to wipe his filthy, gritty mouth. He wiped his nose and lips as clean as possible, swabbed his tongue then, still clutching his moss, struggled to his feet, shaking, and with clothes still dripping. The earth felt firm beneath his sodden feet, his sandals were half on, half off, the fastenings ripped off by the tide. The wind still whipped around him and his rescuers, chilling his wet back and arms. But to stand on firm ground again, he who had been on a heaving boat, struggling in a storm, blasted by the waves – firm ground was wonderful. His toes wriggled in the shingle, feeling the sandy grittiness with joy.

The men who had found him stood silently waiting while he cleaned himself. He was shorter than they were by an inch or so, but then he was buckled over, tired by the force of the waves. He tried to speak but his ordeal had left him exhausted, and also speechless. And although there was comfort in being on land, he was also frightened. Not only by the ferocity of the sea and the tide, but by the memory of feeling a hand on his back, and a push which had maybe sent him out into the deeps? The boat had been small, the weather rough: it could have been the hard thump of a wave. But he wondered. Superstitions were rife among seamen, he knew, and many were not willing to carry a man of faith. This boat crew must have been willing, though, otherwise why would he have been given a place on it? But still … He tried to put the thought aside for later examination, or maybe even forgetting. If that were possible, he thought.

The weather on shore was calming, despite the wind

still swirling about. The sun shone fitfully through the moving clouds, the nearby hilltops were sometimes in shadow, sometimes bright warm green.

He had to live in the present. Silently he called upon Christ for help. And Christ must have heard him, because help was forthcoming. The older of the two rescuers put his arm round Fittick's shoulders and indicated they move on. The other man laid an arm round Fittick's back and by half-carrying the stumbling, nearly-drowned man they got him up beyond the sand and shingle towards a small building. The wooden door opened, showing glimmers of a fire inside. A woman came out, hair gleaming in the sporadic sunlight.

'Oh, my goodness!' she exclaimed. 'What has happened here?'

Her tone was kindly and Fittick understood the meaning at least as well as some of the words, but still found himself unable to talk, struggling with coughing, spitting up seawater. Embarrassed, he wiped his mouth again, looking down at his feet in their ragged sandals.

Raising his eyes again, he looked beyond the woman and saw a number of men and women behind her, crowding out of the doorway, standing along the wall of the hut and watching him. He was clearly the centre of their attention, held between his rescuers, clothes sodden, filthy hair and face and stinking of vomit.

'Fell overboard. Or so we think,' said one of the rescuers, hand on Fittick's shoulder. 'Big waves got him.'

The other rescuer pointed to Fittick's dripping cloak.

'Just look at his clothes. Look at that rope wi' knots in it. Looks like a priest to me.'

The woman interposed.

'Maybe he is, maybe not. What he *is* is a man that needs a bit of looking after. Up to the big house with him.'

Despite the similarities between Irish and Scottish Gaelic, Fittick still failed to comprehend all the words. But he did understand the friendly tone and the smiles and gestures accompanying it. He tried to smile back and bowed his head.

The first man took his arm.

'This way.' And he led him towards the entrance to the round hut, a building of stone and thatch. Fittick, still shaky, stumbled to it with help, and got to the door, stopping just inside to gaze around, looking at the bed spaces round the wall, then the central hearth, surrounded by cushions, where a warm fire was kindled with bubbling pots standing on a couple of trivets. The smells were delicious, even to a seasick man. The pots were being tended by three women, lightly clad in long tunics, kneeling, stirring, sipping. Round the hearth, several men were standing, elders by the look of them, he thought, gazing at their greying hair and air of authority. One or two others were seated by the fire. They all looked round at him as he was ushered in by the older woman, and his two rescuers. The expressions seemed friendly, smiling, welcoming. A couple of the men came towards him, hands outstretched. The women waved their spoons at him in some sort of greeting, he thought. He felt the warmth in the room, the welcome from the inhabitants and the heat from the fire. They eased his bones and warmed his heart, overcoming the feelings of anxiety, the fearful memory of the huge waves surrounding the boat, blotting out the sky. He could still feel the force of the wave slamming down on the boat, dragging him into the sea, plunging him to the depths. He shuddered again at the thought and the folk round the hearth, well aware and fearful of the sea's strength, looked at him compassionately.

'In ye go,' someone said to him, arm round Fittick's soaking shoulders. The man turned to the folk and raised his voice. 'You can a' see – we've got a near drookit man here. Can ye give him a wee bit of space to sit down and get warm?'

'Aye, first he'll need to change these wet clothes,' someone said, waving him in further. 'In ye come.'

And Fittick was led to one of the bed spaces beyond the central hearth with its welcoming glow and warmth. The second man came after them, a tunic and breeches in his hand. Fittick tucked himself into the space, pulled off his wet clothes, shivering, and rubbed himself dry with a rag handed to him. He rubbed the rag over his wet hair, pushing it back from his forehead and behind his ears. He pulled the tunic over his shoulders and a warm cloak, handed to him by one of the rescuers, over the tunic. Then he yanked on the breeches, revelling in the warmth of the entire outfit. Dry and warm. And apparently among friends.

Feeling like a new man, he turned and walked over to the central hearth. He was hungry!

A young woman stood up and beckoned.

'Over here,' she called.

Fittick moved over to where she stood.

'Sit down!' And she pointed to the leather cushion near the blazing hearth. Gratefully he sank down and held out his hands. A warmed bowl of something savoury was passed to him, and a bannock tucked into the gooey mess. The others, watching him, now began to eat, and he ate too. It was a long time since he'd had any food. On the boat, of course, but maybe it had been yesterday, even yesterday morning, perhaps, because the sea was so rough, food didn't get cooked, nor stay in bowls if it had been cooked, nor did many even of the hardened sailors want to eat in such conditions, with the big swell tossing the boat up and down.

He supped and supped until the bowl was cleaned, and more was offered him. Finished at last, he looked round at the circle and smiled, bending his head slightly. He pointed to himself.

'Fittick,' he said.

The circle looked with interest. A tall grey-haired man, in breeches and tunic, stood and held out his hand.

'Angus!' he said. Another grey-haired man, warm, too, in his long tunic, pointed to himself.

'Finn.'

Fittick repeated,

'Finn.' And round the circle they went. Aidan, Drostan, Brude, Urgust, Unust. And then the women chimed in. Aislinn, Brianna, Eithne, Seonaid. He repeated each name and smiled and bowed, though he was struggling to keep his eyes open. The journey, the desperate swim, the storm, the new people, the warm food …

A touch on his shoulder made him jerk awake. Aidan, he thought it was, was indicating that Fittick follow him.

‘Come, my friend, you’ll need to rest and sleep.’

Fittick followed him to the bedspace where he had removed his wet clothes, and Aidan indicated the heap of bedding. It looked fresh.

‘Sleep, my friend.’ He waited until Fittick had lain down and covered himself in the blankets, then returned to the hearth.

Some time later Fittick awoke to the noise of gentle singing. Tasty smells were again wafting through the big round room and he felt hungry again. But first, he must remember, as a man of God, to say some prayers, thanksgiving for his rescue, praise for his rescuers, and forgiveness for those who might have pushed him. He pulled on his knotted rope, left behind from his wet clothes, and fingered the knots, like beads, reminding him of certain prayers to be said

Unknown to Fittick, Angus and several other men were keeping watch over him. Angus peered over, and saw Fittick at his prayers. His eyes widened, and he beckoned Aidan and Finn to look as well. They too were intrigued. Finn made a sketch sign of the cross to the others, eyebrows raised.

'A holy man?' he asked quietly. 'Like those who have come before?'

Angus nodded.

'His clothes are not of our cloth, nor of our style. It seems he comes from other parts.'

'We keep him?' asked Aidan.

'Or send him on his way?' suggested Finn.

'Aye, wherever it is he's wantin' to go.' Aidan agreed. 'We'll need to know his direction.'

The women joined in the discussion.

'Poor man, he seems so nice,' and a second, 'A wet drowned rat it seems to me.' Another woman said,

'Aye, but look here.' And she mimed a circle round her neck, ending in a cross. 'He's one of those holy men. Like Columba, remember what his men said? Against our worship, our gods, our ways.'

'Aye, but those folk that Columba taught, they were nice folk, and they told us about Columba and his teaching.'

'Aye, they came over here to tell us about the Christian God.'

'Mind you, that they said Columba told of new ways, a new God who liked everybody to be at peace.'

'That's so.'

'A God of Love,' they said.

'Aye, aye, that's the case.' The murmurs were accompanied by nods and smiles.

But there were questions.

'Aye, that might be the case. But is that what we want?'

'Peace? Aye, surely!'

'But not against our own gods.'

'And what does it mean anyway, a God of Love?' There were shaking heads and pursed lips.

'And our ancestors worshipped our gods. Do we want to go against what our ancestors did?'

'No, no.' The pursed lips, head shakes and dismissive sounds went round the hearth.

'What our ancestors did – that's good enough for us!'

'Mind you, though, there's that lot in Aberdeen, the

ones that speak of Machar.'

'We don't know much about them, though. They werena fisher folk.'

There was considerable shaking of heads and pursed lips, and when Fittick came back into the centre of the big room, he was met with questioning looks, and considering stares and even frowns. People were still friendly, or friendly enough. Hands patted his shoulders, and he was made to sit down. But there was a feeling of distance: the smiles seemed forced or were absent, and there was no meeting of his eyes, nor grasping his hand.

Not knowing he had been observed at his prayers he wondered whether something had happened during his time of sleep. Did the others feel anxious about sharing probably limited food? Or were they concerned about having a stranger in their midst? He wondered how best to get the friendliness back. He bowed to them.

'Thank you. Thank you.' Keeping his cross hidden, he held out his two empty hands and again said, 'Thank you. You have helped me live again.'

Some of the group stretched out their hands again to take his. But a small section still stood aloof. However, the frowns were changing to surprise.

‘He speaks our tongue!’ Finn said. ‘He must belong in our land.’

Fittick listened intently as the conversations developed. He was still shaky and feeling battered but slightly better after a sleep.

‘He’ll be Irish, same as Columba and as Machar.’

‘Remember what we heard of Columba?’ asked one. ‘Mind the stories that they tell of him? His wonders that he wrocht, curing people.’

‘Aye! but I dinna believe thae stories.’

‘And remember Machar,’ added another. ‘Those followers of his – maybe we should have listened more.’

‘Aye, the wonders that they wrocht,’ echoed an old crone, hobbling up on her stick. ‘It’s a great thing, that kind of speak. Tells ye a lot.’

A tall young man pushed forward. His grubby tunic reached to knees that poked out of his torn breeches. He was friendly and attractive, and about Fittick’s own age, thought the priest. His sinewy arms held out a welcome, his open hands indicated peace. Dark hair stood on end, and his eyes were clear and caught Fittick’s gaze. His smiling expression was welcoming amongst the gruff and somewhat intimidating gaze of some of the other men.

'I am Mungo, sir, and this is the Bay of Nigg.' He spoke in Irish Gaelic, and, in the same language, asked, 'Is this the best way to speak?'

Fittick nodded.

'I speak Irish Gaelic, and I understand it is very similar to Scots Gaelic.'

'Yes,' Mungo agreed, 'but there may be some differences and our accent might make us more difficult to understand.'

'I am impressed, Mungo, by your language skills! How came you by those?'

Mungo laughed.

'That knowledge can wait, sir. Tell me more about yourself so that I may tell everyone – and let me say, that I am sure you are welcome, sir.'

Fittick seized his chance.

'I am Fittick, sent to tell of Christianity to the Scots after the work of Columba and Machar. The Bishop of Meaux in France sent me.'

Mungo looked at him doubtfully.

'Are you aware, sir, that there is Christianity in nearby Aberdeen, and that we on the shore have made our allegiance to our Celtic gods?'

'I was not aware that I was near Aberdeen, Mungo. And I was not expecting ... to be here, in this place.'

'For where were you intending, sir?'

'I believe further south, sir, maybe Fife, maybe further. The skipper of the boat knew of my destination and on which shore I had to land.'

'I may tell my folk this?' Mungo requested and received a nod of permission. Mungo turned and relayed Fittick's words to the others.

'Ah, so it's no' us he wants tae talk to?'

There were still mutterings, unsure whether Fittick would move on or not.

'To *tell* us? What will that mean? What will he expect of us?'

Mungo turned back to Fittick.

'There may be fears, Fittick, that should you remain here, you may wish to take away the gods we worship here already. And to change our ways.'

'Some of Machar's people came to try that,' came a comment came from one of the gathering.

'Aye, we didna want them.' And the surrounding folk nodded in agreement.

Mungo turned to Fittick to tell him about the attempts by the followers of Machar to introduce Christianity to the folk on the shore.

'He did not succeed.'

'Why not? What were the objections?' Fittick needed to know. Mungo shrugged.

'Many.'

A grey-haired elder – Finn? – stood up and said loudly,

'I worship our gods as did our ancestors. What of them? Do you say that they were wrong?'

There were murmurs of support from some of the people.

'That's right, Finn.' And, 'He must answer that!'

Fittick groaned inwardly. After the battle with the waves, he felt unequal to this challenge.

'All I can say is, good sirs, that for me and many others, Christ reigns! As both Columba and Machar have told us many years ago.' People nodded in understanding. Undoubtedly they knew of both Columba and Machar through meetings with the followers of those men. But no direct word from either of these men had reached these shores of the

Bay of Nigg. Nevertheless, the names tripped off their tongues as though they had been old friends.

'That is so!'

'Columba, yes indeed.'

'And Machar, he of Aberdeen. Building his church where the river forms the crook of a bishop's staff.'

Men and women turned to each other and nodded, muttering the names Columba and Machar, and someone also mentioned,

'Colman. He of Portmahomack. Mind you, Mungo?'

Mungo nodded. Indeed he remembered. He had been there.

Fittick tried to understand and interpret the chatter, the nods, the hand-wavings, and the smiles at each other and himself.

'Mungo.' He was hesitant. 'Do you think there is some interest here?'

Mungo nodded.

'There are a few followers among our local people. But you must remember that here in the Bay we have our own ways, and our ways here are of very longstanding.'

‘I understand,’ said Fittick, ‘and indeed it is not my intention to disturb your ways.’ He paused, fearing to let his enthusiasms run away with him. ‘What I want to do is to make sure that everyone knows of other ways.’ He added, ‘But it is possible I may not remain here. I may not be wanted and may have to go on my way.’

His words were clear to the nearer people in the crowd, especially to the women who had helped him as he stumbled, dripping, into the doorway.

‘We canna turn him awa.’

‘He needs tae bide here.’

‘Mebbe it was meant that he landed on our shores.’

Fittick listened intently. It was unclear whether he would be able to remain – or turned out to find his own way south. He shuddered inwardly at the notion. From a privileged and comfortable position both at home and in the bishop’s training, to this – what could he call it? – it was comfortable enough with warmth and food, but with hard rugged seats, and rough bedding. And to have to move onwards was alarming. Strange land, different tongues. Truly a time of trial, he thought.

The debate continued. Until another older man stood up, one seated opposite Finn, and declared,

'We have said enough! This man has been washed up on our shores – he is a victim of the seas, a victim of the storms. We care for him. We offer him our hospitality. We do not turn him out!'

Fittick turned to Mungo.

'That appears definite, Mungo?' There was a question in his voice. Mungo nodded.

'That is Angus: he is the chief elder, and what he says ... goes!'

Fittick was hugely relieved. He was reasonably safe for the time being, he thought. At least, he could take time to look around and work his ways out of the community, if need be. Slow and sure and careful, he thought.

Angus nodded to him and smiled, and Fittick bowed in return, an obeisance from younger to older, from stranger to leader, from junior to experienced elder. All this he tried to convey and Angus's smile broadened as he raised his hand in a form of blessing.

And at the same time, Fittick, in his own mind, stood firm on the principle of respect, taught him in the monastery alongside the doctrine of Christ's supremacy. Many of the teachers there had been clear that there must be respect for the old ways, the ways of the ancestors. Not to do so would incur serious enmity. Better to introduce Christianity gently and peacefully, respect the ancestors and their worship, and introduce Christ as a friend, carefully and peaceably. Some objected, wanting to raise the banner of the risen Christ and shout His glory. But most elected to agree that gentleness, and demonstrating by action the peace and goodness of the risen Christ, was the best way to introduce His word. How could he convey that to these people, though?

'Allow me, sir, to make sure people fully understand you,' said Mungo with a smile. Fittick smiled back: that was the first step.

CHAPTER THREE

He slept that night again lying against the wall near the door, enjoying the stillness of the surroundings. The floor was steady, the bedspace steady also, as against the heaving of the boat. The rest of the bed spaces were occupied and four young men had to cram their beds on to the floor. There was the sweet smell of heather mattresses mixed with fishing smells and body odour. And there were small noises, of snores, noisily expelled breath, cries of nightmares. But these, though interrupting his sleep, did not disturb him. Fittick was used to sharing both room and bed and found the warmth, the smells and the noises all comforting, especially after his journey on the sea. The bed itself was comfortable, with a mixture of heather, straw and herbs to keep it sweet. And there were coverlets of deerskin to keep it light and cosy. He was warm as he had not been since he left France. In his dreams he remembered waving farewell to his mother, her hair golden in the low sunlight, her tears threatening to spill down her cheeks. She was waving to him and in his dream, he waved back, loving her dearly, reluctant to say goodbye.

Early morning light trickling through the half-open door woke him from his tender dreams. Some of the young men were moving out, probably to fish, he thought drowsily. The others were still sleeping peacefully. Moving gently off his mattress so as not to disturb them, he heaved off his night attire, and pulled on his dried day clothes which someone had kindly left at his feet. He fingered his crucifix again. His morning prayers needed to be said quietly so as not to disturb his companions. But they had to be said. The day had to be blessed to Christ's use. He turned away from his night companions and faced the wall, kneeling by his heathery bed. He pulled out his crucifix, letting it lie on his fingers so he could see Christ on the Cross as he prayed.

His prayers over, he rose, made the Sign of the Cross on his body, and turned towards the centre of the room. The space around the fire was empty of all but one young woman who was stirring a pot on the hearth. The same one as yesterday, he thought. Something smelt delicious. She smiled at him.

'A little?' she offered. She gestured to a wooden bowl and mimed filling it from the pot. He beamed. Hungry? Yes of course. And she was a lovely woman. Not for him, of course, but he found himself thinking of her, her slender arms as she held out the food, the fall of her tunic, belted at her slim waist, and her smile as she invited him to join her, her soft dark hair, her eyes … Her warmth was a glimmer of the life he wouldn't have. Stop! he thought. I must stop! Why am I even thinking about her with my work to be done? But her delicate image remained with him as he turned away.

He moved to stand by the doorway to finish his bowl of porridge. The wall of wood and stones tucked in between the planks formed a cool leaning post. The young cook gazed up at him from time to time, wistfully. The open door offered a way out. It was time to leave the room and her presence, he was sure. Out into the open! Open land, open sea, a foreign country, but one whose earth might become familiar. Smiling, he laid down the empty bowl.

'Thank you! Delicious!'

And she smiled back at him as he left the building.

On his own, he took a deep, free breath. He was alone. Christ was with him of course, Christ as his Master. He had vowed within himself to have no woman, no family. Otherwise how would he serve Christ as fully as he wished?

Drawn to the shore, he passed other smaller round houses, pointed stones thrusting into his sandals, sand crumbling underfoot. Gulls flew overhead across the shore line, out to sea, wheeling, diving, landing with assurance on the waves. He moved towards the sea, peaceful as it had not been yesterday. Grey, blue, still, gently swishing its white-capped waves on the shore. Could that be the same sea as yesterday, with the clamorous, strident, crashing roar that he still had in his ears?

Crisp noises on the shingle behind him caught his ears. Someone following him? Not the woman, he hoped. A touch on his shoulder made him stop and turn. The young man who had helped him explain his ideas to the fisherfolk last evening, now stood behind him. He was smiling hesitantly, and holding out a warm cloak.

'Mungo, sir. Your friend from yestreen. What would you think if we do a bit of exploring, sir?'

Fittick grinned as he took the cloak and pulled it round his shoulders.

'Thank you! A good idea. And I am not Sir, please, Mungo. I am but Fittick. And I want to know a little about you, please! Where came you by foreign languages?'

Mungo laughed.

'I have travelled much, Fittick, and learned much, and even stayed with the monks at Portmahomack.'

He slapped his new friend on the shoulder. 'Let's go wandering.'

'Portmahomack, in the monastery there?' asked Fittick as they headed along the beach.

'Yes, but it did not suit me. The life was too … unyielding.'

'Monastic life can be tough,' Fittick agreed. 'Why not become a priest? You can get about and meet people and preach the Word.'

'Train for priest? No, man, I wanted to come back and fish. But, I tell you, I have warm thoughts of our Master, Christ.'

'So I may count on your support.' Fittick made a statement rather than a question. Mungo did not answer, but guided his friend along the shore.

Their stroll along the beach was, for Fittick, like walking along a stream of light. Sunlight streaked through the clouds, bringing a shining brightness to the shore. It warmed his bones, and better than that, it warmed his spirit. Gulls ignored them, and carried on with their calling and swooping. Some were strutting on the shore, while others kept up effortless flight over the sea, complacent in their knowledge of the waters. Mungo pointed out to sea.

'You can just see some of our men on the small boats

– they're after catching the smaller fish. Further out – see? The sails are set and the boats are after bigger fish.'

'Fishing is a skilful job,' commented Fittick.

'Aye, you need a good knowledge of the waves, of the weather and of the seabirds. Look you over there, far off, you'll see the birds hovering. That's where they'll find the fish today, mark my words.'

'Birds know where the fish are?' Fittick was surprised. As an Irishman brought up in the hinterlands he was more knowledgeable about animals than fish. But he was keen to learn.

'Right, and all ready to dive in and catch. And the fishermen too. they follow the birds and get the fish – we'll have some to eat tonight. And plenty for trade with the farmers.'

'Do you use fish for trading? Market your fish locally?'

'Aye indeed,' Mungo agreed. 'We market the fish in Aberdeen, the wee place over the hills. We offer fresh fish and that dried by the wind and smoked. Look here!' He pointed ahead, uphill, to a big wooden structure ahead of them. 'We dry the fish here, and we smoke them, with the fires underneath.'

Fittick stared at bladderwrack, in a heap beside the

big wooden triangle.

‘It seems you would use a lot of seaweed to smoke the fish!’

Mungo nodded.

‘The women gather the kelp and the wrack whenever they can and heap it up here, so we can just help ourselves when we need to.’

They paused by the wooden racks, thin pieces of timber built together to form a triangle, with fish suspended from the crossbars and small platforms, to be dried by the cold air and wind. And to be smoked and cured by the glowing ashes and embers, with something indescribable in their smell. It was more than the usual aroma of glowing ashes, Fittick thought. Even in Ireland he had not seen anything like this.

Mungo was pleased by his interest.

‘This method is from the north lands, Fittick. We have had many northern fishermen round this way, and they have shown us how they preserve their fish. And the taste is wonderful.’

Further up, the shingled beach turned into a series of slopes, gentle, then steep and with some flat areas to be seen. Mostly green, he thought, with animals grazing, but some of the slopes were fenced in and crops were growing. And half way up the slope, near the animals and near the crops seemed to be another small settlement. He pointed this out to Mungo.

'Are these people connected to the people in the shore settlement?'

'Indeed, yes, we are all kin. But those on the hillside farm as well as fish, and we do business with them, and for them, too, helping trade their meat when we go to try to exchange goods. Fish for meat, fish for grain, fish for skins.'

Mungo pulled Fittick's attention back to plants.

'Look at these,' and he pointed. 'The women collect plants like these for food here.' He pointed to ramsons and sorrel in particular. Fittick pulled a small leaf of sorrel and nibbled it.

'Beautiful taste.' There was plenty of sorrel in Ireland and in France, but even so, Fittick thought he had never tasted anything so full of flavour as that plucked from the hillside on this Bay of Nigg.

'And very good for you to eat.' Mungo followed suit and they moved on and upwards, nibbling. 'We hunt as well, and of course there are the birds' eggs. Fishing though gives us our main food. And grains, barley and some oats from the farmers. As you can see on the far hillsides, the farmers grow grains and we exchange grains for fish. And there is the occasional bit of meat from a cow.'

Fittick pointed to a small berry.

'We have this in Ireland, and we have it in France too.'

'Ah yes, the cloudberry. It tastes good.' Mungo laughed. 'We all like our food.'

There was a scuffling sound in front of them, with the leaves of the bushes moving from side to side. A face peered out from behind a large bush overshadowing some thistles and yet more yarrow. But the face behind the small leaves suffered from major ulcers. It was lumpy, greyish and white, and deeply scarred. The eyes were sunk back in the head, and the lips turned in. Fittick shuddered as he stared.

'Mungo, who??? what????'

'Ah. They're there! Shouldn't be so near the shore.' Mungo raised his voice. 'Go on! Back home!'

'What? who? What's wrong?' Fittick stared back at the bushes.

'Can't you guess? Don't you have this problem where you come from?'

'A bad, a terrible disease?' Fittick asked. Mungo

nodded, reluctant.

‘A local family. It’s a bit of a story. I’ll tell you later.’

A stone from behind came whizzing past Fittick’s ear. Straight into the bushes it went, and there was a painful pitiful cry.

‘Got him!’ A young men Fittick had seen in the house earlier came running alongside Fittick and Mungo. ‘They’ve no business to be back down here. They belong up there – see?’ And he pointed up the hill to a small round house, half-hidden by a sturdy fence.

Mungo’s tone was low.

‘We don’t go up there much. The women take up food for them to cook. They leave the food outside. And we men take up the heavier stuff. The youngsters aren’t supposed to throw stones, but it helps to keep them away from our dwellings. Yourself, you must keep away from the folk inside there. They belong to a small family who travelled and met with –’ His mouth turned down. ‘With ... Oh, how I do not like to utter the words!’ He shook his head. ‘And there is another, a bigger group, further along the hillside. See,’ and he pointed to where Fittick could just make out a couple of small buildings. ‘That’s the beginning of the other people’s houses. We know only a little of them. It seems like, that they came from the Aberdeen area.'

'But cannot return there?' Fittick was deeply interested. 'The only thing that would keep people so separate from others would be the leprosy. Is that it?'

Mungo nodded, sadly, eyes on the shingle.

'Aye, that's it. They were all travellers in the northern lands and seems like, well, they might have caught the disease there. They keep well apart.'

'I have heard much of leprosy,' said Fittick. 'There is much in the Italian kingdoms, I believe. But I did not know it had reached these shores.'

'It's a terrible thing,' Mungo lamented. 'Can't be stopped, it seems. And ordinary folk are terrified. We make these leper folk keep their distance here from us. The ones nearby, up yonder, we know well. But the others away on the farther hillside, we do not know much about. Just that they keep themselves in the houses behind that fence, that is enough for us.'

'But this man here ... behind the bushes ...' Fittick began. The bush moved slightly, as if he could be heard by the monster face behind. But it had gone, surely. Fittick stared into the bush. Were the leaves moving again in the shore breeze? The young man who had thrown the stone was sidling carefully round the clutch of bushes, more stones in his hand. He and his companions encircled the bush but left one area clear, a path leading from the bushes up the hill.

'Aye, they come out from time to time – a bit of a wander, I think. They likely feel a bit closed-in up yonder.'

Fittick was thinking.

'Many do think leprosy is a punishment for sins committed by the people or by their ancestors.'

'Whether this be the result of badness, or bad ancestors, bad dealings and thus a deserved punishment, we do not know,' said Mungo. 'And I am not willing to think like that.' He gazed to the horizon where the sea met the sky, his mouth turned down, his thick brows low over his dark eyes. And he hesitated, clearly reluctant to continue the thought. 'But, maybe, who knows. Is that your opinion too, that bad ancestors cause this, Fittick, my friend? If I may call you so?'

Fittick laughed, and banged Mungo on the shoulder.

'Indeed, indeed, let us be friends. I have much need of such a thing, especially from a man of my own age.' The hearty backslapping, he hoped, would distract Mungo from his question. But Mungo repeated it.

'My feeling is that the living loving God and the risen

Christ would never visit leprosy on a family no matter what sins their ancestors had committed,' Fittick averred. 'But there are those men, and healing women, too, who assert that the sins of the father could be visited on the child. Bodily sins, diseases, unhappiness. There is little doubt that a man's illness can later be seen in his children. After all, our bodies copy things from our ancestors, such as, say our brown eyes, our dark hair. Who know but what they may copy other things too?

'But whether these are for sins committed we cannot tell, can we?' Mungo demanded.

'Exactly my own feeling. You have the right of the matter, there, I do believe.'

Mungo laughed agreement, and in his turn slapped Fittick on the shoulder.

'Friends, aye indeed. We agree.' He gestured to a soft grassy bank further on. 'Let us seat ourselves and look at the view.' He seemed happy to let Fittick go slowly up the hill, and Fittick was happy to be indulged. It was tough for those not accustomed to the slopes, gentle though these might seem to the locals.

'Please go on telling me of the people in the huts on this near slope.' Fittick was still fascinated by the thought of the dread disease so close.

'Aye, well, they belonged here, in a way. But they liked to wander a bit and they were in the northern lands, and something happened there, I am not sure what. But signs of the disease appeared, and they came back to their home place here. They sailed back by themselves – they'd gone off by themselves. And they wanted to land here, go up the hills to their own place.'

Fittick nodded.

'Please go on.'

Mungo hesitated.

'There's a lot more but ... well, the nub of the story is that we agreed to let them bide on here, between our wee community and the farmers. And we all tidied up these wee huts on the hillside so they can live by themselves, and come and go as they please so long as they do not come near any of our settlements.' Mungo drew breath. 'We know them, of course, the man Andrew and his wife – she's called Big Nell, and the wee daughter is Wee Nell. Son is young Andrew. He'd be about twelve or thirteen. And the wee lass, she'd be about ten now I think, was eight or thereabouts when they came back. I think they are all suffering, and we keep clear of them, and they keep clear of us, even though they like a wee wander at times.'

'How do they live?'

'Man, oh man! it must be difficult! They have a wee vegetable patch. She gathers plants. And the women folk here drop off fish – at a safe distance, you understand. And their own farming folk leave them a bit o' meat handy for them to cook up. There's water nearby. Plenty wood for the cutting and firing when it's cold. But it must be hard!'

Fittick nodded his understanding. His thoughts flew to the gospels. Christ had cured lepers. What could a lowly priest do to help? Pray, of course, but what else? Visit regularly while keeping a good distance. He could do no less. But perhaps look for healing plants? ask the women which were the best here? Make potions or salves? Maybe that was something he could learn to do.

Keeping his back to the huts, Fittick stared down the slopes towards the shore settlement where people seemed to be moving around. He lifted his gaze to the sea and its present tranquillity. Yesterday, well! he thought, that was a different story. He slumped back on the grassy seat. Young and fit though he was, he was still tired both physically and mentally from the journey, and his near-fatal immersion into the northern seas. He had been lucky! Or was it blessed?

Mungo gave Fittick a sideways look, noticing his fatigue, but carried on,

'As I said, we drop off food for them every other day, and they have a few chickens.' He shook himself, as if shaking the disease and its dreadful thoughts from his mind. 'Let us go this way, further towards that lower hillside. It is an easier walk for your first day here.'

Fittick was more than willing to move away from the hillside and turn his back on the upslopes where stood the lepers' huts. They tramped slowly downwards, revelling in the glow of the spring morning, the sparkle of the sea and the calling of the birds giving each other messages, no doubt, of food to be found, of dangers to be avoided, and who knew what else.

Down on the shore there was a considerable busyness, of comings and goings, of bladderwrack being lifted, of nets being mended. Mungo touched his arm and pointed down with his other hand.

'There beyond are the women with their nets, see?'

Fittick could see a group of older women, swooping lines of dried tough plant material, through and through, up and down. No doubt but they were creating the strands and knots which made up the fishing nets.

'Only the older women?'

'No, the younger ones take their turn as well. Men and women work hard here. Women as well as men get bait from the shore, they get the limpets and any other shellfish they can find. They get the green stuff to go with the fish or meat. They make the nets. And they collect the bladderwrack for smoking. As well, there are small gardens to be tended, with the growing of special plants for cooking with, and eating, and of course dyeing the cloth.'

'All this and caring for plants and cooking too?' Fittick was impressed. He thought of his mother, whose array of servants ensured she never soiled her hands with cooking nor gardening, and certainly not fishing. He laughed to himself. He was certainly in a different place now.

A haunting sound broke the stillness of the air.

'What's that? Where?' Fittick stopped walking, surprised by the sound of chanting.

'Look! Look yonder!' Mungo pointed. In the distance, at the foot of the hillside, just on the bend as the hill turned from the shore, there was a circle of men and women. Some Fittick could recognise, Angus, the elder for instance. Others were strangers. They seemed to be holding hands, swaying, and some singing reached him. Flowers were in the hair and in the hands of the women, and at a gesture from Angus, he thought, they cast their flowers down on to a patch of dry earth in front of them. And they continued their singing. Then they began to dance, slow measured steps, forward, backwards, sideways, in time to their music, in time with each other. The music was haunting, the movement rhythmic, and the whole experience, even at a distance, almost drew him towards the circle, riveted by their presence.

He walked a little nearer, but Mungo stopped him.

'Not too close.'

'What is this? A special rite?' asked Fittick.

Mungo nodded.

'Our Well has dried up recently, and we needs must coax back to life again. Pull back, let us move away, otherwise …'

Fittick finished the thought.

'It is private. Of course. But tell me, how long has this Well been dry?'

Mungo considered.

'I have myself taken water from it recently. Two, three weeks or so? Maybe more, I am not sure. There are other springs, but this is our closest Well and it is a special Well, and we need to get it up again.'

'Special?'

'Let us get back to the house, and we can talk.'

They turned back along the hillside towards the large settlement, glowing in the sunlight. He could see it clearly. Just up the shore from the sand and shingles, settled on the start of the hillside, were the small rough-hewn wood and stone buildings, built near but not too near each other. Surrounding the larger round house, these all stood in the midst of small areas of vegetables. Further off were fields of barley and probably oats. Sheep on the hillside, cattle on the flat land at the top. He wanted to explore the whole area and learn its history, its use, its settlements.

If the well had dried up, whence came the water to help the growth and quench the thirst of the beasts at least, and man too? He stared round but could see no other well in the distance, nor none nearby. Yet the land was green, the crops looked fertile, the beasts looked good and healthy, and well-fed. Mugo had said there were other springs. Water must come from runnels in the hillside. But these might dry up too.

Not everything could be seen at once, he reminded himself. Doubtless there was more water nearby. He tucked the Well into a corner of his mind. There were other things to consider.

His musings continued as he walked silently alongside Mungo. How many people lived here, and would he be able to bring the Christian message to them? And would they permit him to do so? He had to tug in his mind to remember the prayers and the teaching from the monastery. The surroundings were new, interesting, slightly scary in their strangeness, and his efforts to make sense of where he was, and who his companions were to be, pushed other things out of his mind. He felt under his collar for his crucifix. *Christ has died, Christ has risen!* He murmured the prayer over and over to himself as they walked, reminding himself why he was there. Maybe the fall from the boat was important – maybe this was where God meant him to work, to build on the work of Columba and Machar.

He remembered again the many discussions in the monastery: Christ to be foremost! Yes indeed, but let us always be respectful of what is present in the minds of those we want to convert. Respectful? Of pagan gods? Yes, because they have served their purpose for the customs of their believers. We cannot destroy them, nor push them aside. We must go gently. And they might even be features of our own true God.

He well remembered the debate, and he had been on the side of those who wanted to go gently in preaching the Christian message. Only sometimes, he knew, his enthusiasm got the better of him.

His musings continued as Mungo and he reached the

shore and walked towards the settlement. A shout made them turn round. Someone was waving to him. Was it the young woman who had fed him? She was beckoning.

'It's Seonaid, she'll have made more fish soup,' Mungo said eagerly. 'I'm a great admirer of Seonaid's cooking!'

Fittick grinned agreement. But, he thought, it wouldn't be difficult to move from liking her cooking to liking Seonaid herself. He felt her attraction strongly. It was not unknown for priests to marry, he mused, but he wanted to remain a single man. How hard would that be? And, adding to his confusion, it looked as if Mungo was also attracted to the woman – love the cooking, love the woman? Could that be so, wondered Fittick. How would others, especially Mungo, feel about an outsider's interest in one of their women? Thoughts scrambled through his mind. Seonaid. Mungo, a new and good friend. Should he make sure he kept the new friend he had made in Mungo? Or maybe marry, and lose a friend, and, more importantly in his view, he would lose the opportunities of taking Christ and His Word wherever possible. Or, of course, he could remain single, and move to proclaim the risen Christ wherever he was called to do so. And maybe this is what he should do, he thought, ideas tumbling round in his mind.

‘Come, eat and drink.’ Seonaid mimed the actions. He smiled. Indeed, he was hungry again, and the food had been good.

‘Thank you,’ he said in his Scottish Gaelic. She smiled.

‘Come!’

He laughed.

‘I come, indeed, yes, please.’

She smiled.

‘Good.’ And she turned along the hillside, her skirt swishing through the grassy slopes, her hair lifting in the breeze. Had she been one of those dancing at the Well? He wondered about her allegiances. To her kin, of course, but to the Celtic gods? He had detected movements towards the Christian God, he thought.

Mungo accompanied Fittick to the main hearth where a sizzling pot of soup simmered on the fire. A bowl was waiting for them, and gratefully, abandoning his deep thoughts, he picked it up and sank down on to the deerskin cushion. And Seonaid could not have been dancing, he thought, if she had been cooking here.

CHAPTER FOUR

Warmth and comfort, good food, friendship. Fittick tipped his head backwards, the better to look at Mungo, and smiled.

'I feel quite at home.' He beamed on his companion. 'Tell me more about yourself, Mungo, my friend. Before we get on to the story of the Well.'

Mungo leaned back comfortably, stretching out long legs to warm himself at the fire on the hearth. He nodded agreement.

'That I can do for you, though for myself, I fear I am not of great interest. I am setting myself up as a fisherman, and a curer of fish, to dry them and smoke them. This will become the business of my family. It is very interesting indeed.'

'How did this come about? You said 'will' become the business of our family. What mean you?' Fittick's curiosity burst forth in eager questioning.

'Many moons ago we were the victims – I suppose

you'd say – of some raiders. They were fishermen taking our fish from our own fishing grounds. I went with my father and uncle to push them off, deny them the right to our fish. But …'

'Go on!' Fittick sat up eagerly. 'Did you fight them off?'

'Yes! We fought. But there were few of us. And more of them. We were captured, taken on board their boats, and …' Mungo paused, his lips set tight, his brows frowning over his dark eyes. 'We were harnessed to each other and to the oars and made to fish.' Old anger surged. 'Our fish! From our grounds! We needed every one of those for our own families. But…'

Fittick leaned forward.

'You were enslaved, then?'

Mungo nodded, his face grim.

'Yes, that is what happened.'

'There is no need to continue. I would not have asked if I knew there would be such distress.'

Mungo shook his head.

'No! No! the memory is bad, yes indeed, but we did escape eventually. They took us back to land and kept us in a sort of camp. We had to help with the fish caught and, well, all sorts of things they demanded. Building, digging – but working with the fish was best. And I must say there were some clever ways with their fish, which we learned and which I plan to use for our own benefit.'

Fittick was impressed at his strength.

'You must have been a very young lad. What happened? Were you freed?' His words trailed off, as he remembered his own scatterbrained and dreamy time growing up, free to hunt as he wished, and riding deep into the beautiful Irish countryside.

'No, we escaped, and that's a tale for the telling. We hid, with some others, as they knew the area. But enough of that. There is much that I wish to forget.' Mungo laughed. 'I was but fourteen, I do remember, and captivity was …' Mungo's mouth turned down as he searched for a description, '… unbelievable! But we made use of it, all of us slaves. We learned things, and I use my learning now. I learned other ways, and bits of another language.'

This was a man of maybe his own age, thought Fittick, one who had experienced dangerous and frightening times, and had, somehow, survived.

Mungo stood up, stretching and yawning.

'The valuable part of being a slave, as I say, was learning the curing, to treat the fish by smoking with different smells, that improves the flavour and preserves them also. We then had a goodly load to exchange for meats with the local farmers. And I took the knowledge back with me.'

'So some good came out of this,' Fittick said gently.

Mungo nodded. He sat down again.

'That structure I showed you, with fish spread out, that was what our captors did. And as well, I have travelled somewhat around our own lands. The journey back, after our escape, roused my curiosity. My father and I went exchanging foods, bargaining, seeing new places, and for a time, we were guests in Portmahomack, at the monastery.'

He turned to his companion with a grin.

'Enough about me!'

'Then tell more about the Well?' prompted Fittick,

'Aye, the Well. The water is supposed to have healing in it. We can drink from it as well, when we're passing, but there is something very special, a special way ...' Mungo hesitated and Fittick glanced at him curiously. What was coming here? Mungo continued. 'It's what we call Unspoken Water.' Fittick nodded his understanding and Mungo went on, 'When someone is sick, someone mebbe injured, hurt in some way, then a sup of the water, a wash down with the water, then maybe there's some healing. But we have to be careful, though, not to speak a word after we have taken our water, not until we reach home. We have to say our prayers silently, and many do, to the goddess of water.'

'Ah, I see! A Holy Well.'

'Holy indeed. Come out and see.' Still clutching his bowl of soup, he led the way back out of the house, and pointed over to the site of the well. 'Do you see that path above the dancers?'

Fittick nodded. He could just see a narrow line across grassland leading on beyond the Well, turning about the curve of the hillside.

'That is the path where the living cross the land of the Well. Further down, do you see another?'

Fittick nodded again.

'That is the path along which we carry our dead to their final resting place.'

'So the Well is a sacred place, between the living and those going to their eternal rest?'

Mungo nodded solemnly.

'That is a sacred area.'

And no doubt the reason for silent worship, thought Fittick. He had heard of unspoken water before, where the water was taken from a well thought to have special properties, because of its closeness to death and the afterlife. The mystic identity created by this placing was believed to offer special properties to those who drank of its goodness. Fittick understood such water to have special healing, both spiritual and physical, but sometimes when such healing failed, some thought that the pilgrims who asked such help might have failed in their own beliefs and practices. Fittick was unsure about that.

However, if this Well had dried up, did that mean that the locals had failed in their devotions? Fittick was inclined to the pragmatic belief that some rockfall underground caused the stoppage, but the thought of rising water and rising Spirit was intriguing him. He kept to the pragmatic for Mungo.

'Perhaps it may be a blockage of some sort?'

'There are those of us who claimed it was a sign from the gods, but some of us have investigated the ground. We've worked away at the earth, we've crawled about on the ground, poking into the hole, trying to dig other holes.'

'Maybe a prayer to the Risen Christ might help?'

Mungo nodded agreement.

'I suppose anyone who has had dealings with the Christians near here would expect them to want to … help.'

Was Mungo avoiding the word 'interfere'? Fittick wondered, and indeed, that word had come into his own mind. But the important thing was the water and the Well's working. Water was health-giving, bringing the goodness of the earth into man. And not just the practical goodness of what lay in the earth, but the spiritual gifts of water, as God had said '*Let the waters bring forth swarms of living creatures.*' The clarity, the liquid movement of the water brought up from a well gave man pause for thought and much meditation.

He hoped he could help. But how?

As if he could hear Fittick's thoughts, Mungo turned to speak.

'So, if we have not found a blockage, do you think there is a special sacred meaning, that the water will not flow?'

Fittick gazed at the shore, the seabirds swirling, the waves splashing. For once, it was empty of people, and it looked magnificent. But Mungo's question hung in the air. Fittick pondered. There must be a certainty here, no hesitation, but a clear positive answer. He stared out to sea again.

'Water, such water, from the earth, is sacred, Mungo. It comes from the depths, it is pure for us to drink, to wash with, to use as we need. It can give us wellness in living and also great healing.'

'But,' began Mungo, 'why then did the gods – ours – yours – not keep it flowing?'

'Maybe God felt it needed us to pay attention, to help in its release. Who can say what the will of God is?'

'And our gods?' Mungo demanded.

'As to your gods, I cannot answer, but my belief is ...' Fittick hesitated. He wondered if this was going to make sense: he was not even clear in his own mind yet. 'My belief is that with so many people working together to release the waters, there is the presence of God connecting people one to another.'

'Is that really godly?' Mungo asked.

'I think so … people, a community, a togetherness, for a good purpose. I believe there is a spirituality in this – connectedness, I think is a good description.'

Mungo glanced at him.

'You mean a friendship?'

'More than that – strong feelings and a connection for a major purpose. A belonging. To our God, to your gods, and thus, to each other.' And he asked, 'Who might your god be?'

'There are those who think Dana, the goddess of water from Ireland. They invoke her help. And others who worship Brigid, their own goddess of water here.'

'Water is a powerful spiritual element indeed, for your gods and for us. We are connected in this belief,' Fittick agreed. 'And another connection between people and the depths of the earth, with life and living well.' He continued, 'At the beginning of the Bible, God's spirit first moved over the face of the waters, and He said, "*Let the waters bring forth swarms of living creatures*".'

Mungo was impressed.

'Water with many connections.'

'Yes, indeed, connections,' Fittick repeated. 'We connect in so many ways.' Connection was one of his favourite ideas. People connect with each other, yes, but importantly with Christ, and through Him, with God the Father. And thus, they belong – to Christ, and God, and to each other. A whole, a unity, he thought.

'I suppose we used it in so many ways,' Mungo commented. 'I can tell you only a little. I have mentioned the paths already. The pathway beneath the Well is where we carried our dead beneath the wellspring of the fountain. They were blessed by droplets and were near the goodness of the earth, shortly to join that earth. But no longer! We still carry our dead along that path, but there is no water blessing for them, no reason to believe that the earth will welcome the bodies.'

'There was purification on the way to burial when the Well was flourishing,' Fittick clarified.

Clearly the Well had been a vital point in the lives of the small shore settlement. And as if reading Fittick's thoughts, Mungo continued.

'Others made use of the Well, too. The settlements on the hillside, and those from further over, in the small village of Torry, they all came to drink of its water, to fill their flasks, to carry the water with them. And to use it in their healing. But now it is no more.'

His words tailed off in a wail of sorrow. Fittick gently patted Mungo's shoulder.

'Let us pray over it,' he suggested. 'Shall we walk to the Well now? Maybe the dancers have finished.' His idea was to survey the scene and to bless the Well.

'Yes, we can do that. I will check to see whether the dancers have really left.' Hope rising, Mungo headed off towards the well site. Fittick crammed the last handful of bannock between his lips, and saw that Seonaid was at the doorway of the house. He took up Mungo's bowl and his own.

'Thank you!' he said, 'thank you!' Her hands touched his as she received the dishes, with a smile of acknowledgement. He felt again the frisson of excitement which her touch had brought him before, and he pulled his hand away abruptly. She gazed down at her own hand as he moved away from the house to where Mungo was waving to him.

As they moved along to the Well Fittick could see that there was no water bubbling up from the earth. It was still dry and there was no one around. And the paths above and below the Well were empty of people.

'Come on! On we go!' Mungo's words were hurried, and anxious. 'Let's get there before anyone else appears.'

Fittick clutched the hidden crucifix to his heart as they walked over the grass to the edge. He walked round the large hollow, rock-lined, stony and dry. He looked down into it. He knelt beside it, his hands flat on either side, his forehead touching its ground. He was in touch with the earth, in harmony, he hoped, with its life. Again and again, he bowed to the hollow, hands and knees on the earth. Fittick's eyes were closed, his face intent.

Was he praying? Mungo thought so but could hear no words.

Then Fittick stood tall, his hands upraised, his face turned to the heavens. He cried out loud:

'I ask permission to bless this Well.' His voice was strong in the open air. 'I ask that it may bring forth its water from the earth.'

No one was nearby to hear, but the words and their intentions were loud and clear. Mungo blenched, nervous.

Fittick repeated his words. He lifted his crucifix on high as he spoke, and holding it upright with both hands, he circled the Well.

'Hear my prayer, Lord God of Hosts. Thank you! Thank you, O Living God. And Your Holy Son, Lord Jesus Christ!'

And he came to a stop by the path leading to the settlement. Again he held his crucifix high, again he turned his face to the heavens.

'Blessings of the Lord Jesus Christ upon you.' He raised his voice again. 'Blessings! Blessings!

Blessings!' He made a huge Sign of the Cross over the opening. Then he lowered his crucifix, bent his head and prayed silently.

Mungo stood beside him. Unwilling to offend the elders, unwilling to risk his safety and perhaps even his life by disagreeing with them, nevertheless he respected the heart of the belief in Christ, as he had heard it on his escape. And later in his travels he had heard it again from disciples of Columba. He thought he would share with Fittick. Better than fighting and anger, better than curses, and better than the jealousy as he knew these all to exist within the small settlements about the Bay. We should be able to live in peace and to share, he thought. Would that this might happen through the goodness of this man, this stranger washed up on our shores. Could it be that this is the purpose for which he was sent to us? Love, peace, goodwill to all men?

Fittick rose and repeated his blessings, and falling on his knees again, begged,

'Water! Water from this well. And we will dedicate it to Jesus Christ, the only begotten Son of God.'

Again, Fittick raised his crucifix. Again he sketched out the Sign of the Cross in the air above the earth's opening. And again, as he lowered the crucifix, Fittick bent his head in prayer. And again, he begged for water.

Mungo did likewise. Though not sufficiently learned or trained in the Christian way, he at least knew enough to beg Christ to hear Fittick's request.

A splashing, gurgling sound made him raise his head and open his eyes. He gasped. A small spurt of sparkling water leapt from the opening in the earth. It grew taller and larger. It created a big arc of water, so tall that Mungo had to stretch his head to see the top of the new fountain. It sparkled in the sunshine, and drops and rivulets of water splashed over the path beneath and ran down the short hillside.

Mungo gasped.

'Look! Look!'

Fittick lowered his crucifix.

'Water! Water! Thank you, holy Christ!'

Mungo clasped his hands and repeated in the local tongue,

'Thank you, God of the Christians, thank you, Lord Jesus Christ.' He turned to Fittick, wiping his eyes. 'I have seen a miracle! You have worked wonders.' He stammered the words.

'Not I! but Christ in me!' exclaimed Fittick.

Could this be so? Had Christ really worked such a

miracle, so that again there was water from this well? They stared at the falling water.

'This must be holy water,' Fittick said at last. 'Your gods decreed it long past. And Christ has proved it. The dead will be carried again beneath this Well. The living will pass above. There will be connections here between the living and the dying and the burial. This Water is of universal goodness and thus blessed. We will savour its beauty, and it will heal. But we must not taint it with words. We must meditate in peace.'

And so saying, he withdrew from Mungo and sat on the hillside, head bent in prayer, hands holding the crucifix to his lips.

CHAPTER FIVE

Mungo stood before him, head bowed.

'I honour you, my friend.'

Fittick raised his head. His eyes were blurred with tears.

'Honour Christ, Mungo. Honour Christ.'

Mungo stretched out his hand towards the sparkling water.

'Amen to that.'

But there was a shout from lower down the hillside.

'The Well! The Well!'

Finn came roaring up the slight slope, cloak fluttering, hands held with palms upward.

'Our wish has been granted! Our prayers to the goddess of water have been answered. Look! Taste! And see that this is good.'

Fittick braced himself for an attack by Finn. He was sure as he could be that his prayer to his Master had created the surge of water. But clearly Finn thought otherwise.

'Our dance! We have wakened the deeps. Our song! Our prayers! At last they have convinced the goddess of water that we need this Well. And …' Finn continued triumphantly, 'we go on worshipping our own gods. See what they do for us?' And he waved towards the sparkling Well.

Fittick bowed his head.

'Indeed, sir, I honour your conviction.'

This statement was acceptable to the defiant aggressive Finn. But not to Mungo.

'I cannot believe that,' whispered Mungo in disbelief. 'What is it you have said?'

'I will introduce the thought of Christ when I deem it to be the best time. I do not want nor intend to cause stress and strife.' Fittick was trying his best. He was pleased to watch Finn's delight, but did not want to provoke him. Gently, slowly … But he stood awkwardly beside the Well, wondering what was best to do.

Mungo gazed from one to the other, sensing the antagonism from Finn and the restrained determination from his new friend, Fittick, each of whom believed devoutly in the working of his particular God. For himself, he was inclined to prefer the Christian God's action, since the water appeared immediately after Fittick's prayer. He also wondered whether the stamping around on the ground had released some blockage underground. But what had caused the water to emerge on Fittick's request? Surely that was Christ's doing. Mungo moved along to where Fittick was shifting from foot to foot on the path.

'May we now continue on our way to meet those people at the other settlements?' he said. 'The people there are linked with us. We are friends, we marry each other, we consult each other. I would like to introduce you.'

Fittick stopped his jerky movements and smiled.

'And in doing so, my friend, you may, please, teach me more of your particular phrases so that I may also link with you all.'

Mungo laughed.

'Me? A teacher? I will do my best.' And he began the way towards the small houses, relieved to leave Finn.

The going was rough. It had been rocky and uneven

over the shingle but on the way back over the grass Fittick found it bumpy and slippery. He was not as fit as he used to be, he thought. Life with the Bishop in Paris and walking the even paths of that glorious city had softened him. He paused now and then, to allow Mungo to point out special plants, and repeat the local words for them.

As they neared the small settlement on the hillside, there was a shout, a screaming yell. To the left they saw the gesticulating, jumping figure of a stocky man, in breeches and cloak. They could just see a head covered with a whitish cloth, and with holes where the eyes might peer through.

'Aah me, 'tis the leper, Old Andrew. Again! He'll be wantin' something else,' Mungo groaned. 'But what?'

The yelling continued, making sure the leper had their attention.

Mungo raised his voice.

'Andrew! What is it you want? Food?'

'Naw!' The voice was barely human. 'Stop the young ones chucking stones at our fence. They've got me once today already.' And he pointed a swollen hand towards his covered face. 'We've got enough to put up wi'. It frichtens ma wife and weans.

Leave us alane!'

'Oh, my goodness!' Mungo sighed, 'here we go again. The young men want Andrew and his family out.'

'Young men?'

'Aye, the young men, youngsters from Angus's following. And from Alasdair's as well. As you saw before. They don't want the lepers so near. Some of the women feel the same, and some of those from the other fishers, up the hillside, where we're going.'

'What can be done?' Fittick scuffed his feet on the hillside, wondering if the rough ground had any impact on the rough relationships within the different communities.

'Who knows? I'll tell Angus and Alasdair and see if they can keep their young men in check.'

'Bad enough to have leprosy, but to be the object of such hatred also is hard indeed.' Fittick said sadly.

'And there is much fear,' Mungo added. 'Fear of the disease, fear of the folk here. To live in fear all the time, that's terrible.'

Andrew the leper had turned back to his dwelling. Mungo waved at his back, and shouted,

'We'll try, Andrew, we will try.'

The man struggled in through the fence surrounding his home. It shook as he slammed shut the gate. Fittick and Mungo stared sadly at the place. Fittick bent his head in prayer. Mungo turned aside until he had finished.

'Let us continue.'

Fittick nodded.

'What do I say in greeting, please?'

Mungo voiced a short greeting in his Scots Gaelic.

'Hail, elders, hail, people. I am Fittick, from afar.'

Fittick repeated the greeting several times, hoping he could remember it when the time came to use it.

They came to the other collection of small houses on the hillside. Men were standing outside, tunics belted neatly, breeches to mid-calf and deerskin boots tied round the lower legs. Cloaks fastened round their shoulders finished off their morning outfit, for though the sun was shining, the day was cool. Women were moving around, shawls over their shoulders, gathering leaves, picking up kindling, laying up a store of twigs to ensure a good cooking fire on the hearth later. Fittick thought, It is the same everywhere. All over, whoever we are, wherever we are, we need food and we need warmth. Even the lepers, he thought.

The men were staring at him, some with welcoming smiles, others frowning in curiosity over someone new appearing. The women likewise were smiling, nodding and curtseying, and some of them held children by the hand, or with a hand on the head of a child. Fittick guessed that not many new people visited these shores.

'Greetings, good sirs and ladies,' shouted Mungo. 'I bring you a new friend.'

Fittick touched his forehead, and bowed. He in his turn shouted the greeting that Mungo had taught him.

'Greetings in return.' An elder stepped forward. 'Whence came you, sir?'

Mungo translated and then turning to the elder said,

'My friend, Fittick, does not fully speak our language. He was washed off his boat two days ago and has been healing with us on the shore. He is willing to learn our language.'

People smiled at that.

'And,' added Mungo with a pride new after the

wellspring. ‘He is a Christian, a man of God.’

At that there was a stirring among them.

‘Here? A man of the Christian God? This man?’

The women turned to each other.

‘A man has come. A man of God, the Christian God, visiting us?’

Of the men, two or three stepped forward with hands outstretched.

‘From Columba’s men? Or from those of Machar?’ Others remained watchful, in front of their homes.

‘Machar was one of Columba’s monks, Fittick. He built his church in old Aberdeen.’

‘Indeed, yes, I know of Columba and of Machar.’ Fittick bowed his head.

‘We welcome you. This is the settlement of headman Alasdair. That is myself,’ said one man. ‘We welcome you most sincerely.’

‘But not all of us agree with the Christian God,’ said another.

‘However,’ added a third man, ‘you are welcome here so long as you keep your God to yourself, or to those who are fully interested.’

Fittick's eyebrows rose at the knowledge there were some of his faith in these people. So I shall be welcome amongst some, he guessed, and careful of others.

He decided to say nothing of the Well, but Mungo was full of the news.

'The old Well, it has returned. It is bright and sparkling as new. It can again be used for …' and he paused.

'Healing, no doubt,' said an old woman standing beside chief elder Alasdair.

'Indeed, yes.'

'How did this happen?' Alasdair asked. Mungo described Fittick's actions and words. He indicated the crucifix under Fittick's shirt, and many stared in surprise. Fittick had no need of words to tell him of their feelings. Their looks indicated surprise, some fear, hostility, perhaps. Fittick raised a hand.

'It may also interest you to know, my new friends, that there was a stamping song and dance before my own prayers.'

Mungo nodded, not surprised that Fittick had acknowledged this circumstance. And Alasdair himself looked pleased, whether at Fittick's prayers or news of the stamping dance round the well,

Mungo could not say.

'Whether it is our own, or the Christian God, it matters not. The water is indeed most welcome. We have much need of water, for all purposes. Our own godly rites, of course, of healing, and of just thirst quenching.'

'But this sounds perhaps miraculous?' commented the old woman standing beside Alasdair, looking at Fittick. He understood her.

'It has emerged from underground straight up to the sunlight. It has passed roots and rocks to get here, and it has all the goodness of the Earth in it. That in itself is miraculous.'

Mungo intervened, and pointed to the Well down the hill, where the clear crystal water was leaping into the air.

The elders stared, the women gasped and pointed, and the children began to run down the slope towards the water.

'Stop them!' cried Mungo. 'This is holy water.'

Fittick laughed.

'The children will do no harm. It will be holy when we pray and fill our flasks, and meditate. Let the children play.'

CHAPTER SIX

It was a grand walk to the Well in the later part of the day, crunching along the stones and shingle, the sea hishing in their ears. As they neared the Well they could see its sparkling water leaping into the air, reaching into the darkening sky. Finn was there with his followers.

Angus stood tall by the side of the Well and greeted Alasdair and the group of fishermen.

'Look! Look at that!' Alasdair pointed. He shivered, as if the hairs stood up on the back of his neck. 'Water now! Where there had been none! What has happened?'

'Aye, aye, we can see.'

'That's the Well as we used to know it. Beautiful, just!' And Angus stretched out his hands to catch drips of the sparkling clear water. 'Man, it tastes good.'

'It is good water,' said a voice from behind Alasdair. Fittick appeared to take his place by the Well. 'It is water straight from the earth and its healing properties. And I have blessed it, with words of God and His Son, Jesus Christ.'

Ouch! He'd done it again. He'd opened his mouth without thinking, without checking his audience. He angered some of the men beside him.

Several turned on him, Finn being one of them.

'Witchcraft!' he shouted, brandishing his long stick. 'Witchcraft! You are not welcome here. This Well is for our gods only.'

The band of young men stood beside Finn.

'We worship Brigid, the goddess of the water. We worship Dana, the Irish goddess of water. They take us close to the spirits, they help us care for our world, they tell us of all that is and was and will be.'

'Aye! Brigid! Aye! Brigid!' others chanted. 'Dana! Dana! Dana!'

'And Mannan, our god of the sea and what's in it,' added one.

'Aye! Mannan! Takes care of us fishing.'

'Aye! Mannan!'

'Mannan! Mannan! Mannan!'

‘Cailleach! Cailleach! Cailleach!’

‘Beira! Beira! Beira!’

The shouts roused the sleepy seagulls who flew into the air squawking and screeching.

Finn shouted again, rousing them.

‘This is not of our own knowing. This is from our ancestors and will be for our children.’

‘Aye! Brigid! Aye! Mannan! Our gods and our goddesses!’ The chant from the young men led them forward to confront Fittick, fists clenched, eyes glittering, and jaws thrust in menace.

‘Away wi’ you! Away wi’ you!’ Finn was howling now. It had all gone wrong so quickly. Fittick stood, helpless before them.

Angus stepped forward beside Fittick.

‘That was not well done, sir priest,’ he said in a low voice.

‘Blessing the water might have been a quieter announcement,’ said Mungo fiercely. ‘You have stirred up trouble here.’

Indeed he had. He mumbled an apology, condemning himself inwardly, remembering his monastery admonitions to watch his too-ready tongue.

Someone from behind the antagonistic group flung a stone. It just missed Fittick. But another followed that hit him in the shoulder. He clutched his shoulder, dropping his crucifix which then dangled at the end of its chain.

Finn leaped forward and pulled at the crucifix.

'Wrong! Evil! Foreign gods!' he yelled. 'We have our own gods! Let them be!'

His followers surrounded Fittick, striking him on the back, the head, the buttocks and the legs. Fittick ducked his head into his hands, his neck hurting badly with the pulling of the crucifix cord, and the blows raining on him were merciless.

Mungo fought his way through the assailants to help Fittick, despite his anger with his friend. Angus was on the priest's other side. But Fittick did not see them. Others joined Mungo and Angus, fighting with fists, their own sticks raised against the attackers. Several men fell. Others staggered off holding their heads, or arms, injured from the furious blows being dealt.

'Is this how we welcome a stranger?' yelled Angus, grabbing at Fittick's arm, pulling him away from the centre of the fighting.

Gradually the fighting ceased as men fell, were

injured or even, maybe, moved by Angus's words.

Fittick stood, horrified and contrite.

'I am sorry … I am so sorry … sirs … to bring this on you. Let me leave and leave you in peace.' He stumbled off a little way, aghast at what had happened, but Angus and Mungo followed him, protective. Finn's men retreated too, breathless from the sudden fight.

'There can be no peace while Finn is like this,' Angus sighed, dusting his hands, pushing back his sleeves to inspect an injury. 'Were it not your good self, sir priest, there would be something else.'

'But maybe not so bad,' Fittick said.

Angus laughed.

'Oh aye! He wants my place. Wants to be the Big Man here but …'

'He has not the knowledge,' Mungo said quietly. 'He is not good with the fishing and knowing where to go. Nor is he easy with other people.'

'Methinks he is unwell,' Angus suggested. 'He used to be an easier man.'

Mungo agreed.

'I know Eilie thinks so, and Seonaid too. He is even

rough with the bairn.'

'His anger grew fiercer when wee Alys's mother, Finn's daughter, was taken from us,' Angus informed Fittick, who was still shaking from the ferocity of the fighting. He was a peaceable man, who had seen little anger and fisticuffs even as a youth.

'My Bishop told me to be careful,' he said. 'If Finn is ill, then of course I forgive him. And I must find some means of making amends.'

There was a cry. The men turned round. Seonaid came running towards them.

'Finn said he had dunted you good and proper, sir priest.'

Fittick was immensely touched by her anxiety, and fumbled to answer her. Mungo stepped in.

'Not so,' he answered with a grin. 'We are still here and standing.'

The other men laughed and straightened themselves.

'Look at the Well, Mistress Seonaid,' said Angus. 'That's what we came to see.'

Seonaid looked and gasped.

There had been anger and fighting, injury and fear.

But the water surged clear and sparkling, pure and innocent into the sunlight, and dropping in a wide arc to the sloping ground below.

'We can now carry our dead underneath.' Seonaid pointed to the big arc.

'Indeed, and use the water for healing again, too.' Fittick was still keen to offer despite the anger he had aroused.

'It was always a healing well,' Angus pointed out.

'But think about it, Angus,' said Mungo. 'There were some folk saying that the healing prayers were not always answered. That folk still suffered. Despite all their use of the water.'

Fittick watched Mungo, impressed with his assurance as he spoke with Angus. For himself, addressing a headman, senior priest, and bishop had required considerable nervous thought. Though he had been such a short time in the small fishing community he had noticed of all the young men Mungo was the foremost in welcoming, helping, and talking to the head elder. A distinctive man, with character formed through enduring and escaping slavery, perhaps.

Angus nodded to Mungo.

'Indeed, yes indeed, that was the case. There were

some frustrations. So, Fittick,' he turned to the priest. 'You think there could be more healing? From your God? Say on.'

'I will bless the Well and ask for healing in its waters. And then it will be as Mungo described it before. Anyone who wants will take a drop in their hands. Or they will fill a flask. While the water is in the mouth or being carried to the sick person, then there must be no speech. It must be a meditative journey, with prayers for the sickness and recovery.'

'Aye … I just mind that. Or something like it.' An old man had followed them to the Well. 'And if you put a coin in, that will help as well. The body of the coin turns up to face the top – then the sickness is in the body. If the head on the coin turns uppermost, then the sickness is in the head.'

'Magic?' Fittick queried. Angus and Mungo grinned at Fittick's expression.

'We have many beliefs here, sir priest, friend Fittick!' laughed Angus.

'But there is much we have in common, Angus,' said Fittick. 'My prayers and the prayers and beliefs of your people are close.'

He would ask soon to tell of his beliefs and his meditative prayers, asking for help, asking for care and cure. And the focus always on God and His Son.

With Mungo on one side and Angus on the other, he turned back to the settlement.

CHAPTER SEVEN

The joy Fittick had felt as he heard Mungo joining in his Christian blessing, and in the restoration of waters, was soon diminished. The hostility towards himself was certain, to judge by the experiences at the Well. And the fisherfolk were in the right of it, this was their home. He was an interloper, a stranger to them, they had a right to be suspicious. In his own opinion, undoubtedly God had to be heard, the risen Christ acknowledged – but in the fullness of time, in the goodness of heart, rather than in any belligerent exchanges and in any sort of combat. Had he not heard of this in the monastery? Some of the teachers had insisted on forcefulness. Others had suggested gentleness and the acceptance of other ideas. And he had thought the latter had the right of it – but he could not stop himself when he felt the power of God in him.

'A bit homesick?' asked Mungo, settling down beside him in the big house. 'I know a bit about that from my own experiences.'

'Just a bit! I would be pleased to converse with my colleagues and teachers about these matters, ask them how to do better,' Fittick acknowledged. 'I have so little experience.' He lapsed into silence, thinking over his preparation for travel, his debates with fellow students. This was more than debate, though, this was the real thing.

Not only these deep matters, but the shouts and cries of the lepers on the hillside, their fears, and their sufferings, preyed on his mind. All his study and prayers had not prepared him for these.

Outside called to him and he moved towards the door, leaving Mungo seated at the hearth. Fresh air, slowly darkening sky, seabirds calling. The shore was busy. Women were helping with the nets, the fish were being pulled from the nets and tossed into baskets to be carried to big stones, where they would be scrubbed, filleted and maybe put on the big drying racks Mungo had shown him. The women's kilted tunics, tied to allow good free movement, their sleeves pushed up, their strong arms working ceaselessly, picking, throwing, shaking the nets, all this was new to him as a son of a fine lady and gentleman, a scholar and an intent Christian. This was real living, he thought, maybe as Christ had known it. From sea to hearth to bowl. With the work of human hands, constantly moving, the mind thinking. He had never seen such a sight, not even in the peregrinations with other young monks, when they had fastened their cloaks, mounted on asses, walked or rode with enthusiasm to the hills to worship, to the communities to preach. He grinned to himself. What could he have known then to give to these communities? The risen Christ, of course.

But how to show His might to a heads-down community, working to keep themselves alive? And with little time to spare, he remembered, for just sitting and listening. How to bring Christ's ministry to them, to tell them of forgiveness of sins, to tell them of His love and compassion? Would they think of their own sinfulness in terms of Him or just in terms of hurting each other? How could he talk of love and compassion to such hard-working and poor people. To tell them, ask them to think of their own sinfulness, as well as their own need for love and care. Sometimes, he thought, we just bring them words. Only words. But there must be love there, the deep love of Christ for mankind. The feeling behind the words was necessary. Giving a warmth of soul to those who had little time or energy. How could he demonstrate that feeling?

How to show the hope that there was in Christ's living and dying and in His resurrection?

A shout from behind made him pause. He was about to start his stroll up the hillside, but someone was calling to him.

'Nae there. Nae there!'

He looked round, bewildered. It came from one of the fisherwomen. She was shaking her head.

'Not up there. Go along that way if you want a walk.'

A movement on the hillside caught his eye. Was that the headman of the other community hurrying along? - no doubt to talk of the Well. Was he to wait on the man coming along? He mimed a question of the fisherwoman. She shook her head.

Another shout caught his attention. Mungo came hurrying up.

'Not up there, Fittick, my friend. Not now. The lepers are getting restless.'

Fittick shook himself free again.

'Christ healed a leper.'

Mungo laughed.

'But ... you're no' Christ. And even if He did heal a leper, this is a family, it might spread again.'

To Mungo's relief, Fittick stepped back.

'True! True! We have the folk here to think of. Not just the one person or two or three. And others nearby. But tell me more of them, Mungo. You have told me how they came back with the disease. And a little of what they did. But more please! The sadness and anguish of a life left behind, to deal with this horror of leprosy – what is that doing to them?'

'Andrew was a fisherman, and kept a few beasts as well. His wife, Nell, I said she was very good at making beads, and Andrew got the shells for her, they washed them, crushed them up, she did the beads and made them into necklaces and so on ... keen to build up that kind of trading, I think. That's one thing that got them travelling around.'

'So – how do they come here, on this hill, so near your own community?'

'Well, it was this way.' Mungo settled into a long comfortable stride. Right along the shoreline, gulls wheeling, calling. Shouts from the shore the one to the other. A happy, busy community, thought Fittick, measuring his stride with Mungo's.

'They sailed back from the north lands. They'd done their trading, but ...' and he paused, 'there was a something ... a something about the man's face that made us on the shore not very happy.'

'So?'

'We waved to them, said what's up, what's wrong? But they insisted on coming to shore and tied up their boat. We kept away from them and we got Angus to tell them they were not welcome with us, and to get on back to their own folks up the hill. And off they went.' He pointed to a rough pathway in the distance.

'And how did you find out what was wrong?'

'Simple. Angus called on their headman, and the headman said, "They're not here. They're over there." And he telt Angus, "We're no' sure if we want them".'

'A couple of miles off,' Mungo pointed. 'there was a couple of wee houses and there they were, and they had built a fence round the houses. And you could see, even from a distance, that they were no' right looking. Scabs on the face, bumps on the cheeks. They didna' look good at all. And the headman told Angus that though nobody said the word lepers, that's what they were all thinking.'

Fittick was silent for a moment. Then he asked,

'How do they live? What medicaments do they have? What help is there?' To himself he was thinking, they can't be abandoned, someone must help here.

Mungo was continuing his talk.

'We only go up the hill here at sunrise or sunset and

they know to keep away from us, stay in their huts, don't come out past the fence. Usually. And the women from their own old people and ours, and from Alasdair's followers, leave food and drink, sometimes made-up stuff? And sometimes just the bits and pieces to make up a meal. They have water, lots to drink.'

'From that Well?'

'No, from the wee rivers on the hillside. But then, they will go out and get their own water, and sometimes their own plants.'

'What about medicaments?'

'Well,' Mungo hesitated. 'I don't know much of that. You could ask Eilie or someone else.'

'I have heard that plantains are good for rubbing on the skin,' Fittick began. Mungo shook his head, denying knowledge. 'Dandelions, wild garlic, plantains, yarrow?'

'Ask the women.'

'They make potions? Yarrow butter?' He recalled medicines his mother had talked of.

Mungo groaned.

'Fittick, my friend, ask me about fish. Don't ask me

about plants!’

‘Does someone rub the stuff on their skins? Maybe the mother to the children?’

‘I don’t know! We’ve been told to keep well away. I don’t know what the family themselves might do.’ Mungo made a feint, towards the sea, away from the leper house.

Fittick understood and laughed.

‘Walk on! right to the end of the shoreline.’

And up on the hill, a man and young boy watched. Their faces were swollen, their lips trembling, drool and spittle running down their chins. There was sadness in their eyes, and a fear. But a shout from inside the fence made them turn back.

‘Come in, come in. The wimmin will be coming up with the dinner. Keep awa.’

The fence gate swung shut. Facing it was an older woman, her face likewise scarred, but the young girl with her was beautiful, unscarred, pale skinned with long bronzed hair. Had she escaped the dread disease? or was she carrying it inside? Her family wondered. She had tried to escape the huts, to get to the shoreline, to meet others. But she was too well known to be accepted, and regularly she was turned back.

More shouts came from the hillside and a barrage of stones hit the fence, making it shudder and tilt. Old Andrew swore under his breath. He picked up a rock, and banged the fence posts back in, while young Andrew, his son, propped them up with some big stones that had come hurtling across.

'Unclean! Unclean!' the raucous shout echoed round the hillside. 'Unclean!'

'Wait until it's darker, and we can pick up some food and whatever is left for us,' the wife cautioned.

Fittick, moving further along the shore, turned to gaze back up the hillside.

'They are sinful, don't forget!' A memory of the Bishop's voice sounded in Fittick's ears. 'Leprosy is a sign of sin!' The two lepers he had glimpsed had gone, back into their fenced dwelling, he thought. Ugly, disordered and distorted, and thus corrupt in the body. And in the soul? Never! What sin had this family committed? Or were they carrying the sins of others on their own bodies? He found it hard to believe that a loving God would create such misery for people.

His heart was no longer in his walk.

'Back home?' he suggested to Mungo. But though the shore settlement was beginning to feel homelike,

Fittick carried in his heart the sight of the leper family, their yearnings and their fears. And above all their isolation.

And these were not the only ones. There was a larger colony of lepers on a further hillside.

'We leave them to the Torry folk to help out by way of medicines and drinks and food.' explained Mungo. 'We've got enough to do wi' our ain folk here.'

Two leper colonies on this shore area. Fittick decided he would visit the nearer one often, and find out more about the others, whether he could help them or not.

CHAPTER EIGHT

In a wee house near the main building, to which he and Mungo had been invited, Eilie murmured something to Mungo. Fittick could not hear. He looked at Mungo who shrugged and spread his hands out, indicating, Fittick thought, 'leave it to the women'. Probably something to do with his dishevelled appearance, thought Fittick ruefully as he smoothed his rumpled tunic again. Eilie pointed to it and smiled at him.

'I would like to mend that for you. Tonight perhaps.'

'Thank you!' Fittick was delighted. She smiled again and turned to the hearth. Her kindness soothed some of the anguish he still felt, the memory of the lonely suffering family on the hillside.

'Would you like something hot to eat and drink before retiring?'

It had seemed a long time since the last meal, and at the thought of food, Fittick realised how hungry he was. He nodded enthusiastically.

‘That would be most welcome.’ Mungo joined him by the hearth fire.

The women were muttering to each other, exchanging glances as Seonaid stoked the hearth and Eilie stirred the pot of soup simmering on the embers. Fittick glanced across the room. Near the back of the house was a bedspace with someone small already lying in it. A young girl, lying on her back, her long golden-brown hair tied back, her face white and quivering as she breathed.

‘There’s something going on here.’ Fittick turned to Mungo as he sat down. ‘Do you know anything?’ He wanted desperately to talk of the lepers, to discuss what could be done, to create prayers round them. But it felt wrong to do so at this moment in the warm room with its kindly hostess, and with a suspicion of something underlying Eilie’s welcome.

Mungo nodded.

‘They’ll be discussing wee Alys, Eilie and Seonaid will. Well-known round here, wee girl, now very sick with a fever. Legs twisted and she canna walk or even move much.’

Fittick touched his breast.

‘My heart bleeds for that child.’ He hesitated. ‘Do

they want me to see her, think you? I know Eilie is a healer and I am not, but … in Christ's name I would pray for her quietly, or openly if that is wished.'

Mungo shook his head.

'I am not sure, Fittick, sir priest. We can but ask. But wait a while.'

Fittick nodded. He turned back to the hearth, and at a glance from his hostess, added some sticks to the fire.

'That is an advance, indeed,' he chuckled. 'To add to the fire, to tend the blaze. That is both practical and spiritual.'

Seonaid warming the bannocks, Eilie stirring the pots – a warm, home-like comfort. Fragrant smells tickled Fittick's appetite and by the looks of him, Mungo's too. Mungo was gazing avidly at the bowl which was being prepared. Seonaid took it, and a bannock and handed it to Fittick. Then she took the next for Mungo. With her own bowl in hand, she sank down close by Mungo, dipping her bannock into the fishy stew.

'Delicious!' breathed Fittick. He felt he had had a tough day, and needed some sustenance. Before he began eating, however, he bent his head, made the sign of the Cross above his bowl, and murmured something in Frankish. Mungo followed suit in Gaelic, and Seonaid and Eilie watched, then also bent their heads to murmur a short prayer.

Fittick watched carefully. The actions seemed sincere, and he felt good about them. But would others here be more defensive? He supped his stew reflectively. It was good. In fact, it was so good that he looked round hopefully for Eilie to offer him more. Smiling, she took his bowl and refilled it.

'And another bannock?' she asked, waving one in front of him. He beamed at her and took it. Maybe it seemed greedy, but who was he to argue with good food when it was presented him? He dipped his second bannock into the stew, folded it, dripping, into his mouth. Plate emptied, he then wiped it round with the remains of the second bannock, and drank some ale.

Well fed, he now felt fit for anything.

'Thank you, God,' he breathed, touching his crucifix. Unaware that others were watching him, he bent his head in a short prayer.

He raised his head. His eyes caught those of Seonaid, questioning him.

'What is it, mistress?' he asked. 'It seems you might want something of me?'

She nodded and gestured towards Eilie.

‘May I tell him?’

Eilie pursed her mouth.

‘I suppose so,’ she muttered. ‘Go on.’

Seonaid leaned forward.

‘You have not met all the inhabitants of this small home,’ she told him. ‘There is one, you may see her bed … a child … a very sick child … whom perhaps you might like to meet.’ Her voice ended in a question.

‘Indeed, yes!’ Fittick enthused. ‘I may pray for the child, surely, either with the family or by myself. I would like to be of use.’

Eilie’s mouth turned down. Maybe she was thinking of what her husband Finn would say? Fittick wondered. Or maybe she preferred her Celtic gods and goddesses. Or was she upset that her own healing had been unsuccessful? He waited.

Seonaid turned to Eilie.

‘May I take him to meet the bairn?’

Eilie looked down at the ground.

‘Maybe,’ was all she said. Seonaid looked at Fittick.

‘The bairn is sick, very sick, and Eilie, my mother, is the good wise woman caring for her.’

Mungo repeated Fittick’s remarks.

‘Fittick wants to know what is the matter? And what do you do for her?’

Eilie turned away, tears trickling down her cheeks.

‘I can do nothing! Nothing!’

Seonaid said,

‘It is her granddaughter, and my niece. My sister’s daughter. She is four years old and very sick of a fever. And her legs have got twisted.’

‘And none of Eilie’s remedies seem to work for her,’ Mungo added softly. ‘We all know and have been watching and hoping.’

Eilie picked up two jars, one with a golden liquid and one with a green liquid.

‘These are of fennel, rosemary, and sage, sir priest. I dose her with a drink of each every morning, noon and evening. And I have used the water from the Blessed Well. These have not alleviated the sickness though they have diminished the fever.’

Fittick asked,

‘How long has she been sick?’

Eilie’s shoulders hunched.

‘She’s been weakening, ever since ... ever since her parents died. She had a bad throat for a whiley. She’s been off her food, sleeping badly ... Then her legs are not strong, they’re twisting.’ Eilie’s voice choked in her throat, and Fittick put a gentle hand to touch her sleeve. She gulped. ‘Her parents ... were ... drowned. And I fear we will lose her, too.’

‘May I see her?’ he asked again, gently. This, he thought, was why he had been invited into Eilie’s home.

Eilie raised her head, her mouth now firm. She touched his arm.

‘Follow, please.’ And she turned away from the hearth and across the small room to the nest of bedding he had seen earlier. The child lay uneasily, hair tousled, face white, arms twisted, legs likewise as Eilie pulled the sheet away. Fittick knelt beside her and felt her wrist, and her neck. He laid his hand on her forehead. He opened her eyes, gently with forefinger and thumb. He laid his right hand on her head and bent his own head in prayer. Eilie stifled a sob as she joined in. Behind her, Seonaid did likewise.

A cough from the door behind them made them all turn. Fittick got up and moved away from the child. Finn was glaring at the company.

'What is going on here?'

'She is sick! She has been sick for weeks. As you well know.' Eilie stepped forward. 'And she is *my* granddaughter, Finn, as well as yours. And I care for her. And,' she added fiercely, 'I will get help wherever I can for her.'

Finn scowled at Fittick, growled,

'This is *my* house as well. She is *my* grandchild too. Just remember, just remember!' He turned on his heel and left the house, as if he expected everyone to obey him at once.

Remember what? Did Finn have special authority over the child? Fittick wondered. To pray for her to the local gods?

Eilie's tears seemed to have disappeared. She turned back to the little girl, biting her lip. She was angry.

'Tell Fittick her name?' said Mungo, forestalling Fittick.

'She is our little Alys. Our dear little girl.'

Fittick looked at Seonaid.

'And had your sister other children?'

'No, just this wee darling. And we love her.'

Eilie's tears were flowing freely.

'My daughter's only child! I have only Seonaid left, if this little one dies.'

Fittick stepped closer towards the bed space.

'Permit me, please. I would like to pray with her.' He dropped to his knees by the bed, and held Alys's thin wrist. Bowing his head, he touched her wrist with his cross and intoned a prayer. Her hand lay limp in his grasp. But she shuddered and twisted her upper body, trying to drag her knees up to her stomach. He laid a hand on her small body. It felt very hot to his touch.

'May we wash her with the water from the Well?' he asked.

Mungo picked up a pot from the hearthside.

'May I fill this?' Eilie nodded, and Fittick added,

'Remember! Do not talk! Either on the way there, or the way back. It is Unspoken Water, remember.'

Mungo ran off to the Well - fast!

Fittick turned to Eilie.

'You are a wise woman, you know your healing plants. But have you asked for help, too? From – ?' and his voice stopped.

Eilie wiped her tears away.

'Indeed yes, sir priest. From all the gods and goddesses I know.'

'Then may I add Christ to your own prayers, strong as they will be from a grandmother's heart?'

She nodded, hands crossed on her heart. And they waited.

Mungo reached the Well in minutes and held the pot underneath the falling water. He ran back carefully holding the full vessel, finger to his lips, not speaking, though men shouted to him, and women asked what he was doing. He would not talk, as Fittick had told him. It had to be Unspoken Water. In the house, he handed the vessel to Fittick.

With one hand, Fittick raised high the pot of Unspoken Water. He held his crucifix in the other hand and raised it to the level of the pot. He brought them together, and intoned words of prayer. His stillness and intense focus filled the house with such a strong presence that the others stood back, mute.

Again Fittick held the humble pot high as he could, clutching the crucifix in his other hand just above the sick child. He called out:

'Christ! We ask You. You have said if we believe, we will receive. And whatever we ask in prayer, if we believe, we will receive that which we ask. We ask You now to bless this child, and heal her.'

He repeated his request.

'Christ! Only Son of God. Bless Alys and heal her. This we beg of you.'

He lowered the pot and crucifix to place them at the head of Alys's bed. And he began praying, softly this time, again for the healing of the child. Then he dampened the cloth.

Eilie made to speak, but he touched his lips with his fingers, signifying silence.

He drew the blanket and clothing from the child, and began to stroke her gently with the dampened cloth. She moved her head from side to side. He continued wetting the cloth and stroking the child's body. She stirred slightly as he drew the cloth over her face and neck.

Eilie stepped forward, alarmed. But Alys sank back

again into her apparent slumber. Fittick continued the gentle pull of damp cloth over hot body. As he did so, Alys moved a little, sometimes her head, sometimes her shoulders, and twice she moved her arms.

Then he paid close attention to the twisted legs. He tried wrapping the cloth round one leg, and laying both his hands on the legs, prayed gently,

'Saviour, this good child, this beloved child – you have said that whatever we ask you in good faith, you will do. We ask now, Eilie, Seonaid, Mungo and I, your faithful believers and followers, spare the life of this child. Love her and care for her as you were loved and cared for as a child. Bring her back to her loving family.'

There was no movement, no sign of any change at all. Alys lay still as she had before, stertorous breathing, occasional twitching of limbs. He must wait. And hope, if he was allowed, to repeat his healing process and the prayers.

The breathing seemed to stop. The little body was still.

The eyes closed. Fittick could see no rise and fall of the small chest. He groaned inwardly, head bowed. Had he failed? Had Christ failed him and the child? No, that was impossible. He would try again - later.

CHAPTER NINE

He turned to Eilie to explain, but she was beside her granddaughter, stroking her, patting her, and covering the still body warmly. She laid the damp cloth on Alys's forehead. Seonaid patted it into place, singing softly to her small niece as she smoothed her hair.

'Does she ... is she …?' Seonaid questioned Eilie who shook her head, and continued patting the small body.

'Sing to her again, Seonaid.'

Seonaid sang, the gentle childish songs which Alys loved, which her mother had sung to her. Eilie continued patting. Both women were weeping.

Fittick moved back from the child, back towards the doorway, followed by Mungo. The two women were so absorbed in the child's comfort that they did not notice the men's leaving.

'Let it be,' murmured Mungo, sensing Fittick's sadness. 'Who knows the depth of the stillness and darkness. It may be healing.'

Fittick shook his head, eyes on the ground and mouth turned down.

'It does not look good. She seems ... not to be breathing.' It was a harsh admission, and the words stumbled out of his mouth, as if unwilling to be uttered.

Eilie came out after them.

'Thank you for what you have tried to do. Who knows what may help?'

'Let me try again, please,' begged Fittick. 'These things are not always solved by one effort.'

Eilie shook her head.

'Indeed, Fittick, you may try, but I fear … I really fear the worst.'

They re-entered the hut where Seonaid was still by wee Alys, singing, stroking, soothing.Eilie looked at the bairnie and shook her head. She turned back to Fittick.

'Let me give you some ale.' Eilie picked up a jug of warm ale and poured some into a beaker. She handed it to Fittick and gave another to Mungo.

'Drink, please.' Her voice was cold and her body

tense, as if she were ready to run fast. Her thoughts were clearly on wee Alys, lying so still by the wall of the room.

They drank, standing. Neither of them felt sufficiently welcome to sit by the hearth, nor, in fact, were they invited to do so. Seonaid and Eilie seemed to be no longer at ease with their visitors.

Fittick blessed his ale before drinking and heard a sob from Seonaid.

'It did not work, your God did not heal her.' Her hopes had been high, of an immediate miraculous cure, and Fittick, remembering Christ's miracles, in particular the healing of the paralysed man, had also had high hopes.

'Christ healed many, Seonaid. You may have heard of the story of the man who was paralysed, and whose helpers lowered him down to Christ's presence, down through the roof. Because there were so many queuing up for healing. If I may, I will try again now.'

Eilie nodded permission, and he went over once more to the small bed. Kneeling again by the child, he prayed, holding his crucifix over the stillness of the small body.

'Christ, be with us. And heal this child. Help this

child, we beseech thee. In the name of Your Father, Christ, hear us.'

Again he picked up the pot of water. He dipped his fingers, one by one, and raised them high above Alys's head. Light from the doorway illumined the drops as they dripped on to Alys's head. Then he dampened a cloth with water from the pot, and again he stroked Alys's hot, tired face with it. He drew it round her throat, he wiped her arms and hands, and lastly, laid the damp cloth along the twisted legs. He who had no children, who had no younger brothers or sisters, who had no dealings with the young, he seemed to know what to do, by instinct or by God's grace.

He wetted a clean cloth and held it to Alys's mouth, wiping her lips. She moved her head. Her little tongue came out and it seemed that she licked the cloth and tasted the water. Her eyelids fluttered.

'Water,' she whispered. 'Water.'

Seonaid was standing beside him. She turned back to the hearth.

'Eilie! Eilie! Alys spoke!'

'But one word only,' Fittick said. She did not hear him. All her attention was on Alys.

Eilie came fast from the hearth. She knelt by her

granddaughter and slipped a hand under the small head to raise it gently. Her eyes were intent, her body tense as she gazed at the tiny child. She gestured to Seonaid.

'More water, more please. A few drops in the mouth.'

Seonaid wetted the cloth again and dripped a little into the half-opened mouth. The child swallowed and said,

'More.'

Seonaid tilted the flask again. Eilie gave her a little more, and set the flask down. She sank back on her heels, hands to her face, weeping.

'She lives! She lives!' Tears flowed down her cheeks. Seonaid was shaking, her sobs choking her throat, gazing down on her small niece with a love and tenderness Fittick thought he would never forget.

Meanwhile, he prayed silently, and behind him, Mungo stood with his head bowed, and his right hand tracing the Sign of The Cross on his own body.

'If she lives, will she – what will she be able to do?'

Fittick's thoughts ran round in circles. Movement, yes! Drinking water was one thing. Good. But real movement? walking?

Wait and see, he told himself, and returned to his prayers.

The silence was thick with meanings, hope and fear, love, and memories of Alys's parents. They waited, it seemed for a long time, and for what they waited they did not know.

And then, piercing the silence, breaking the stillness, there was a sound, the sound of the child crying, whimpering. And there was some movement. One leg was thrust out, the other still curled under but they could all see muscles moving in the tiny leg. And the arms were moving slightly, up and down, hands no longer in a tight fist, but stretching open as though Alys was trying to use them. She began to cry, with shuddering sobs.

'Dear God. My God! It is a miracle.' Eilie spoke reverently and sank to her knees. Seonaid followed her and both made the sign of the Cross. Mungo knelt at the child's head. He too bowed and crossed himself.

The sobbing increased. Alys's eyes opened, deep brown and troubled, and stared about at the adults surrounding her. She stretched her body on the bed, her legs straightening out. Her arms moved upwards from the bed, reaching to her grandmother. Her mouth opened in a wail.

'I'm hungry.'

Eilie collapsed on to the bed, head buried in the covers, and wept, her shoulders shuddering with the intensity of her sobs. Seonaid likewise was weeping, but upright, her hands out to catch the hands of her niece, her mouth pursed in a kiss.

'She lives! She lives!' Eilie's sobs took the form of words. 'My little one, my blessed darling, she lives!'

Seonaid flung her head back.

'Thanks be to Christ! Thanks be to the One who cured her. Thank You! Thank You! Thank You!'

Mungo was speechless. His eyes were damp, his mouth open, but he could not utter a word. He was rigid with the enormity of the action. This child, twisted, lame, sick, thought to be dying – this child moved, cried, straightened her limbs. The man of God, his arms and hands held out over the bed, the drops of Unspoken Water, had created this miracle. What he had witnessed was a miracle. He thought it must change his own life.

Fittick laughed. His tension had eased, and his face was now alight with joy. The cry of a child! Her movement. Reaching out, stirring, wriggling, child-like. His prayers had been answered. God and Christ had heard him and responded. He repeated to himself:

'The Lord has heard me!' And he stood up and shouted, 'Thanks be to God!' It echoed round the small chamber and the sounds reached outside.

And the others echoed him.

'Thanks be to God!'

Seonaid raised herself, hugged her mother, and went dancing out of the door.

'She lives! Our Alys is recovering! Thanks to Fittick's God.'

Fittick groaned. He should not have shouted, but his delight was such that he wanted to reach the heavens with his gratitude. But what would the worshippers of the local gods do?

Eilie touched his arm.

'Leave her to me, now,' she whispered. 'And come you and sit by the hearth.'

He hugged her, united with her in the delight of the child's movement. And for him, he added in his mind, rest was good, rest and be thankful. The concentration had been hard, there was huge effort in focusing so intently on Christ and his words, bringing the image of Christ into his mind. And pleading with Christ the Saviour for mercy.

He moved to his allocated seat and fell back against the cushions, thinking hard.

Meanwhile, Eilie sat by the child, smoothing her hair, talking to her, and feeding her with sips of warming porridge. And sips from the pot of blessed water. Alys half sat to receive these, then lay back again, contented. Her eyes were clear and bright, her colour warm. And the fever seemed to have left her body. It seemed that her legs were too frail to support any weight, but they could move from side to side, and she could lift them, a little, up and down. Eilie encouraged her.

'Up one leg, my little one.' And Alys, grinning, raised one leg. 'Down again!' And plonk! Down went the leg. 'Now the other leg,' coaxed Eilie. And the movement was repeated. The legs were straight, they moved when required. Strength to bear weight would come, Eilie was sure, as the child continued to improve.

Eilie remembered a few years ago when followers of Machar in Aberdeen had come to the shore. She had loved then the sound of the new God with His Son, Christ Jesus, a loving man, a caring man, a man of peace. But it was not a popular view. The men, the elders, preferred the other gods, gods of thunder, noise and warfare. Or so it seemed to Eilie. But their prayers to Christ had been answered. And answered well with the child beginning to eat and drink.

A sound from the doorway made her turn, and Alys's head turned also to that opening. Finn stood there, scowling.

'Whit's this I hear?'

Eilie put her fingers to her lips.

'Hush, she is recovering, but needs no loud noise.'

'Recovering? What do you mean?' He lowered his voice slightly, but the child shuddered against the vibrations.

'Fittick said his prayers, and washed the child with the cloth wetted from the well, water which he blessed with the name of Jesus Christ. And she woke. And began to move. And she has taken a little food, something she has not done for days.'

'I suppose you think that this Christ cured her? I say NO. I say witchcraft!' Finn was thundering again, and Alys began to cry.

Eilie patted her.

'Hush my baby, don't cry. Finn!' And her tone became commanding. 'You must leave this house if you are going to shout. I shall come with you and explain our happenings. But here, the child must have quiet!'

Finn's expression was ludicrous. He was not accustomed to being so vigorously commanded by Eilie. Even though the house belonged to her, he should be the one in charge, he was the man and an elder.

Ignoring him, Eilie moved back to the hearth to poke in a few sticks to keep the heat going. Then she stepped outside, and waved at him to follow. Her voice was cold.

'There is no witchcraft going on here. You must not use that word again.'

'Must not! I, your elder, your husband, must not? Do I hear correctly?'

'Yes!' Eilie snapped. 'That child has suffered enough, and the Christian God has helped her. We will be thankful, all of us, for the intervention of this God, this Jesus Christ.'

'By the spirits of our ancestors, we will abide by their gods.'

'This child has lain for weeks without eating, with little movement, and with a fever. If the Christian God and his Son can help, we must take it and thank them.'

Fittick and Mungo exchanged glances, and moved back from the hearth, edging towards the doorway, hoping to escape. This was no quarrel of theirs. And then Seonaid appeared.

'I agree with mother. Alys, your granddaughter, Aisling's child, is now moving and eating. See.' And she pointed into the house to the bed, where the child, still lying on the mattress, was nonetheless smiling, with her eyes open and gazing at her family.

Finn hesitated, but being defied by Seonaid overcame his hesitation. He turned on her, shouting,

'You are no longer welcome in my house! Leave immediately.'

Seonaid gave a gasp, and a flush of anger rose in her pale cheeks.

'This is my mother's house as well as yours. And you are my father.'

'I will be no kin of yours!' snapped Finn and turned to walk away from the house. He barely noticed Fittick and Mungo, edging towards the doorway. Fittick fingered his cross again.

'The way of the Lord can be hard,' he said to himself.

Eilie came towards them.

'Come back, come back,' she said. 'You must stay in this house for tonight at least, sir priest, and perhaps, Mungo, you might want to accompany him? Who knows but we might want more prayers? I shall watch over Alys, of course, and Seonaid might be keeping me company.'

The two women seemed little upset by Finn's anger.

'Mother Eilie,' said Seonaid, 'go you and talk again with Finn. As her grandfather, he should be pleased with Alys's recovery.'

'And will you watch over Alys for now?' asked Eilie.

'I will, and these men will do likewise. I feel sure she will be well.'

Alys lay on the mattress, breathing easily and evenly. She had kicked off her covers. Her colour was better, her legs stretched out, maybe a little curved, but straighter than before. She opened her eyes as they stood watching her. Frowning, she opened her mouth into a square, ready to scream. Seonaid came in and bent over her, and the scream was stifled. She knew Seonaid. This was safety, this was good. She smiled instead.

'Little love,' Seonaid said tenderly, 'my little niece. You are getting better. You are going to be well.'

Alys smiled, not really understanding, but pleased

with the warmth and attention of her beautiful aunt.

'It is thanks to these men that you will be made well.' And Seonaid gestured towards Mungo and Fittick. Mungo shook his head.

'No – it is thanks to Fittick.'

And Fittick, in turn, said,

'No – it is thanks to God and His only son Jesus Christ.'

'God?' said Alys slowly. 'Christ?' She sighed, and closed her eyes again.

'Good. The child sleeps. We will leave her in peace.' Seonaid tucked the soft deerskins over the little girl. Fittick admired her soft voice, and the care she gave to her niece. He also admired, but pushed aside, the beauty of her figure as she knelt and covered the infant, stroking her hair. Seonaid's own hair fell loose over her shoulder, and the firelight lit up the glinting red strands in the brown. He sighed. Women were not for him. He turned away, trying again to erase her image from his eyes and mind as he had done before.

A move to the fresh air would help, he decided, and as he stood outside the door, he marvelled again at the beauty of the scene. In the early dark, he could see the sea washing gently against the delicately coloured sandy shore, with its pebbles, its seaweeds and the gathered boats on the shore. Small wooden and stone houses huddled together above the high tideline. There were families all along the shore, despite the darkening sky. Children played round about, gathering seashells, he thought, judging from their triumphant yells of discovery. A smell of fish came up from the shore as well, and he could see people in the last of the light bending over a pile of fish, skilfully slitting and boning them. The pile grew higher.

Turning, he moved inland, up the gently sloping green hill to its rounded top. Cows lowed to one another, shadows now. On the hillside was the next settlement, and just to the right of those houses he saw the Well again. A blessed well, and water, a spiritual as well as a healing drink.

In the morning he would search for monoliths for which the people in these lands were famous. Perhaps they were hidden in the trees in the far distance. Perhaps tucked in the dips of the hillside. Fittick himself was by way of being artistic, and he wanted to see the special carvings of these people.

There was a touch on his shoulder, and someone stood beside him. Startled, he came out of his reverie, and turned to greet his companion. Mungo stood there, smiling as he too surveyed the peaceful scene.

‘A goodly land, a Godly land.’ Fittick broke the silence.

Mungo only nodded as he gazed round at the beauty of Nigg Bay.

‘Here, we might build a chapel.’ Fittick pointed to a flattish area, halfway up the hillside.

Mungo stared at him.

‘It would not be allowed. Many elders of these families would oppose the idea. Yet …’ He fell silent and Fittick watched his expression change from negative to one of considering an idea. ‘Maybe so … at the moment, yes. But when word gets around – and it is starting to be heard – that Alys is better, then you may find a more friendly attitude than exists at present.’

Fittick smiled.

‘I like the idea, but I too have some doubt. As yet.’

The two men laughed as Fittick pointed up the slope.

‘Those cows may well hinder any chapel being built. Do they belong to these people on the shore, or are there others nearby?’

Mungo swung his friend round to face south.

‘See there? Within these hillocks lies the Vale of

Tullos, and there you will find the cows' owners. Not fishermen like our men, but farmers, with animals and fields of oats.'

'So the meat is traded, is it? For fish, as you have said.'

Mungo nodded.

'Just so. And I see that even a man of God is interested in commerce!'

'A man must eat!' Fittick protested. 'Feed the body, feed the mind and feed the soul. All are important.'

'Aha! Then let us go and feed the body, right now. I know that Seonaid is warming a drink for the bairn and for all of us.'

CHAPTER TEN

Next morning, seated once more at the hearth, able to gaze towards the space where the bairn lay, Fittick took his cup of warm liquid. It smelt … interesting, he thought, as he took a delicate sip. It was hot! And the flavour was something he did not know. He turned his head to ask Mungo, but Mungo was drinking steadily and did not notice the enquiring look. Seonaid did, however, and asked,

‘Is your drink to your liking, sir?’

Fittick sipped again and said truthfully,

‘It is somewhat unusual for me, demoiselle Seonaid. If I may ask, what makes it thus?’

Seonaid laughed and said,

‘It is a form of mead, sir, brewed from our local honey, and steeped in warm water, kept warm by the hearth. It is very good for you.’

Fittick raised his cup.

'Thank you. I will drink with pleasure.' And he quaffed the liquid. He had had mead to drink before but nothing quite as strong as this seemed to be. After finishing it he felt snug, and at once sleepy again, yet lively, wanting to do something but lacking the energy to move. He raised a hand to catch her attention. 'Domina, demoiselle, may I ask?'

She laughed at him.

'That is Frankish, is it not? Demoiselle?'

'Correct!' Fittick grinned. Despite his vows and his determination to maintain fidelity, he was enjoying being a young man joking with a young woman. He was but a mere boy for all his twenty-eight years. Quite tall, was Fittick, and a good-looking young man, whose mother had desperately wanted heirs of his body. But he had refused. His vows, taken when he was no more than twenty, had remained firm. And until now, he had never met a young woman to whom he was attracted. He could only deal with this attraction by calling to mind his vows to serve the risen Christ as a single man. However, it was difficult. There was no one he could consult. Brother priests were far away, though he could imagine their responses. Some had taken vows of celibacy, some had not. But for himself, his early vision of the risen Christ, hands outstretched, haunting eyes, held him captive. He could not betray this Master by taking a wife. He stretched his legs in front of him, warming the soles of his feet as near the hearth as he could. Remember! The word rang through his mind.

But there was nothing to say he could not enjoy her company. He struggled to think of something he could ask her, something to keep her talking.

'I was going to ask …' he began.

'Say on.' Seonaid sank down on to a cushioned sheepskin. 'What were you going to ask?'

He wriggled again on his cushion, thinking hard.

'Well, yes, I have wondered about the … about the Well … the water. How old is the Well, how was it used?'

'Why do you ask, sir?'

'I am curious about this place to which I came so suddenly and so unplanned.'

His response seemed to satisfy her.

'It has been set apart, sir, by our good elders, and our ancestors before them. I do not understand it all, but it is said that the water is special, made so by request to the goddess Salacia or Amphitrite, the goddess of leaping spring water, from Roman times. Or so I am told. And there is our own goddess, Bec, and as I have said, our goddess of water, Brigid. And there is Dana, the Irish goddess of water. Also Ogma, he of eloquence and speech fluency. The Well is also linked with Tir nan Og – of which no doubt you have heard.'

'Of course I have heard of Tir nan Og, the land of eternal youth. And a Well with more than one special deity? Thank you, that is all very interesting.' Fittick's mind was working again. 'I think I would like to go back to the Well.'

He had some knowledge of Roman gods and goddesses. And he had certainly heard of Tir nan Og, being the Irishman he was. Were these always to be separate? Or could they be linked with the Christian message of love? And how these might be combined with Christianity, he did not know. Christ was to reign supreme, Christ the supreme ruler of the Church with His father God. These pagan deities and beliefs must be eliminated somehow, yet – could it be, he wondered, that they were all part of Christ, when He was as yet unknown to man in this area? Could it be that all these deities, these beliefs, were fractions of the true, the living, the whole God and His Son, Jesus Christ, who embodied all these beliefs – of spiritual water, of eloquence of speech, of eternal youth, or rather of eternal life?

How he wished he had his priestly companions with

whom to discuss, debate, exchange ideas. How he wished he could talk with his spiritual supervisors, and his spiritual superiors. He looked up.

‘I shall go to the Well. Thank you.’

Seonaid had been planning to accompany him, but his movement was so definite, so determined, that she fell back, disappointed. To her, he was a young man, a goodly man, and she had no idea of his vows.

Fittick walked slowly towards the well, his thoughts in a turmoil. Could he encompass all these ideas in one magnificent God, he wondered? Could he ask the pagan elders to work with him on this? To teach him their ways perhaps, while he taught them the ways of Christ, and His father God?

He noticed the tiny scarlet pimpernel flowers by his feet and stooped to pick one.

‘God’s creation! The tiny, the delicate, the beautiful.’ And another, larger plant. ‘This is the yarrow, my mother has made a tea from it,’ he remembered. ‘It is also a healing plant, and it is also beautiful.’

He stood, face bent downwards, to stare at the plant life by his feet. Pimpernels, yarrow, sage, betony, sorrel, mugwort. There were more. He did not know them all, but what a glorious lore of plant life in this small area.

He raised his face to heaven.

‘God!’ he shouted. ‘That’s it! The plants have the answer!’

With the myriad of special plant life in one area, they created their own place. And the more they grew and the more they were used, then the greater meaning these plants would have. A community of plants, for nourishment, nurture and healing. There was purpose in combining these particular plants, a recognition of their different values and a recognition, too, of the wholeness of in their combination.

‘So might it be with these deities,’ said Fittick to himself. ‘They belong here, in their own individual way because each has a special personal characteristic, with specific meaning for distinct needs. But, but,’ he felt he was so close, ‘they might join with the Living God and His Only Son, Christ Jesus. So that there will be companions in spirit, and the sense of belonging in those worshipping the local gods might expand to belonging with Christ who, in His own good time, will become the only Living God. The preaching of Christ’s way, the spirit eternal, the afterlife with God, and the focus on the unity of mankind, and its union with God, will surely exalt the spirit world of these people and their gods.

‘I have been shown The Way!’ And Fittick leaped into the air with joy.

As he landed, he caught sight of three men coming up the slight slope to the Well, towards him. He groaned inwardly. What had he been doing? What had they seen? But they were grinning broadly as they reached him.

‘Well, Fittick, my man, what has pleased you this bright morning?’

Finn was the pleasantest Fittick had seen in the last couple of days or so. Had something changed in Finn’s mind towards himself, Fittick?

‘We have been talking, my men and I. And women also, of course. And we have decided to ask you to tell us more of yourself and your ideas.’

A second man spoke.

‘That of course does not mean that we will take any notice of them.’

The third chimed in.

‘But you will have your chance. That is all we can say.’

Bewildered, Fittick stared at the men. He could understand most of what was said but there were some unfamiliar words, maybe in the local dialect, which puzzled him. However, the tone was friendly, the action of holding out a hand more amiable than turning away scowling, and the smiles on the faces indicated maybe some rapprochement? Perhaps. He needed Mungo to translate fully and indicate the way the wind was blowing.

So he allowed himself to smile, to touch the hands held out to him, and nod agreement.

'Come you this way,' said Finn, directing them all to the downward path.

'A moment, please,' said Fittick, and he turned back to the well, cupped his hands, and inwardly saying a blessing, drank a small sip of the beautiful spring water.

The men watched him. Then Finn stepped forward, cupped his hands and also drank. The other two followed suit.

And only when the last man had drunk did they resume their downward way.

'We may speak,' Fittick remembered, 'as we have no special healing purpose.'

Mungo was at the foot of the short slope, waiting for them.

'Have you need of me, Fittick, my friend?'

'Indeed, and I do.' Fittick smiled broadly. 'These

men have it in them to be friendly and to ask something of me.' He continued in slight embarrassment. 'They caught me in a moment of joy.'

Mungo laughed. 'Indeed, Fittick my friend, your moment of joy was obvious to many.'

Fittick laughed. His position seemed more secure. He was no captive, after all. He was a rescued man, washed up on shore, speaking some of the local language, and unsure of the customs, and who would grudge him a moment's pleasure in all that misery? He wanted to share the reason for that pleasure, even if it might be difficult to describe.

'It was,' and he was hesitant, unsure of how best to describe his feelings, 'because I had looked round me, seen the beauty in the earth, shoots coming forth, the greenness, their fruitfulness of flower and berry and root and branch. It made me think.' And he paused again, looking at his companion as they walked on, behind the other three.

Mungo indicated the landscape.

'It is indeed beautiful, with the sea and shore, and the hills and valleys, and all the plants. Indeed you are right. A bonny place!'

Fittick beamed at this.

'It made me wonder whether these many plants could – in their way – represent the variety of God's bounty and of God's nature, in that He might allow the many other gods and goddesses to be wise men and women, and to represent different areas of life, as plants represent different tastes, and actions for us.'

Mungo frowned.

'I wonder, indeed I do. You are more like to understand and know these matters than I, but I was taught in Portmahomack there was only one God.'

Fittick wondered who had taught his friend, and how he had learned. Through listening? Through reading? Through discussions and disputations? He must find out more of Mungo's time at Portmahomack.

'Indeed, I would not disagree with you, but my feeling is that in our one earth – and there is only one earth – we have a multiplicity of vital plants. And perhaps within one God, we have a multiplicity of different aspects.'

'Please continue,' Mungo said courteously.

'That does not mean more gods, but some aspect of our God who perhaps offers help in our difficulties or pleasures.'

'You mean that our different gods and goddesses are all part of God and part of the spiritual path to the one true God.'

'Something like that,' Fittick nodded. 'It would need more thinking out than perhaps I am capable of doing. But…' He trailed off. How would he put his next idea, and could he suggest it to the elders of the families?

Mungo prompted him.

'But …?'

'But could it be that we put them together with God and Christ his only Son, and perhaps … make an assemblage such as we have of our plants in our one earth?'

Mungo was bemused. It had been difficult for him to continue to accept that he must follow the gods as practised by the elders of the families to whom he was attached by birth. His obedience to family rules and to his father and uncles was strictly demanded and observed. But in his heart, he venerated the learning he had managed to find first in his captivity, then later on various journeys round Scotland, when he had accompanied his father selling and exchanging fish products for meat, and to buy food for the family at home. And, if he had to be honest, his father and he had enjoyed a little bit of exploring. They had enjoyed meeting others, enjoyed seeing new countryside, the well farmed, well tilled area of inland Scotland. And for himself, he had been intrigued by the new beliefs of the one God and His Son, which he had heard mostly at Portmahomack, in the monastery where he and his father had been guests for a short time.

And part of these new beliefs was that there was only one God and one beloved Son. So how could Fittick even begin to consider more, and call them parts?

He frowned as they walked, and Fittick who had had hopes of Mungo's understanding and even, perhaps, support, was downcast. It had seemed such a vivid, vibrant idea. One God, yes, indeed. And his only begotten Son, of course. But different aspects of them reaching out to help people with different needs – and then again uniting them in the One God.

CHAPTER ELEVEN

The elders led the way to the large gathering at the foot of the hillside just beyond the shore settlement. Fittick saw a circle of stones, with two large stones facing each other at different sides of the circle. Both were heavily inscribed with carved symbols, beautifully cut with vivid and vibrant pictures of significant beings and objects - a mirror, a dolphin. And on one big stone there was … a Cross. Fittick stared at it, stunned into silence. A Cross. Here! Had Columba reached out so far? Had it been Machar, his disciple? How had this come about? He stood hesitantly beside the stone with the Cross and watched as the members of the shore community sat in a circle between the two large, decorated stones. Elders took the inmost stone circle, others sat behind them.

From his upbringing Fittick knew about such meetings, members always seated in a circle. People took their places within the circle, and no one was left behind, or left out. Equality, comradeship, ease of communication – those were what the meeting circle meant, he knew. Pictures on the big stones told stories and reinforced beliefs, reminding individuals of which god to speak to, and how, for offerings and for requests. And the meeting circle was where people could tell what needed to be told. Important events in the community needed to be shared, such as the story of a death and mourning, or the story of a handfasting, with a couple coming together in the sight of the community, and then too of a new birth and rejoicing. And there were also stories of the gods and goddesses and the myths and legends of the ancestors to be repeated, handed down. And within the Circles themselves there was a sense of the sacred, of otherness, of a space and place beyond the here-and-now.

He touched the sculptures gently, drawing his fingers over the carved lines. The vivid beauty of the work took his breath away. Carvings of men, walking or riding, of horses, of a weird beast, maybe a dragon, he thought. And the beautiful intertwined circles and lines. There was no doubt in his mind that the Cross had a significant place on this Portal, in this Circle. Shared space – shared faith? But to come across it so suddenly had taken his breath away. He could only stare at it in mixed awe and delight. Who had carved it? And why? And both carvings were on the one vertical surface. He had heard that where Christianity was represented, symbols for other beliefs are carved on the reverse side. Clearly, this was not always the case.

It must be a sign to him. It must.

'Be seated!' boomed Angus, waving to places round the circle. He took his own place, clearly a familiar spot, and waited until the elders had seated themselves. Angus sat opposite Alasdair and Finn among the elders. Two leaders facing each other, as Mungo pointed out. Other members of the families moved in, some quickly, some slowly, and seated themselves round the Circle. This meeting must be important to the community, before so many people would give up tilling the soil, collecting plants for food, fishing and general home keeping. What was it for? He turned to ask Mungo, but Mungo was standing now in the centre of a small group of elders, gesticulating, and talking rapidly. What about? wondered Fittick. Could it be himself? He bethought him of his Bishop's words,

'Go carefully, go slowly, take time. Our Lord created our new thoughts in a few years, but we must go gently to help others change their minds. Remember, Fittick, though we know the light that shines for us, others may be slower and reluctant to give up that which is familiar to them, which their ancestors loved, and whom their ancestors worshipped.'

There had been times in the monastery when Fittick had wanted to run away. Difficult times, times of learning and struggling to understand the demands of the Lord's will. But there were also times, such as the memories he recalled now, when the Bishop's understanding of humanity and humility encouraged him, called him forward and supported his ideas. And there were times, such as that on the hillside recently, when he felt the presence of Christ within his reach, even within himself, humbling and glorious at the same time.

So slowly does it, he told himself.

A clapping of hands drew his attention back to the Circle. Mungo had seated himself beside Fittick, and all other seats were filled. Families sat together, with men in front and women behind. Angus took charge.

'Welcome! Welcome! All of you are welcome to our circle of belonging! Anam Cara! Anam Cara! Soul's friends!' He turned to his righthand neighbour: 'Anam Cara, Aidan.' Then he turned back to his wife and family: 'Anam Cara.' Others followed suit, and even Fittick was included.

'Soul's friend, Fittick!' said Mungo, beaming affectionately.

Then Angus continued,

'We are gathered here for two reasons. The first is to affirm our own community and beliefs. The second is to ask our visitor about his own self and the beliefs which he obviously carries with him, and which he may wish to share with us.'

Angus subsided with a grunt back on to his cushion-covered stone. Fittick grinned as he himself shifted position. Clearly Angus liked comfort and the stones could be hard.

Someone else stood up – Finn. He began intoning, and one by one others joined in. The chant spread, and as others stood up to join in, the music grew in volume and intensity. Fittick found himself enchanted by the sound. Mungo was standing, intoning also, and the depths and beauty of his voice reached Fittick's ears despite the numerous other voices singing. Then the women joined in, and the song swung round the circle as different sections sang different parts. The beauty of the music went to Fittick's heart, and he bowed his head.

As the music finished and the singers subsided back on their stones, Alasdair stood in his turn, alone, his hands aloft above his shoulders, and shouting,

'Great Gods, Great Fathers, Cailleach, Great Mother, we await you, we listen for you, we want to hear you.'

Someone else was repeating,

'Anam Cara! Anam Cara!'

Fittick beamed. There was a sense of belonging here, of friendship and care. Surely he could build on this? Mungo was translating where he thought Fittick needed help, and Fittick caught the echoes as Alasdair repeated himself over again. The crowd responded,

'Aye, aye, aye!' over and over again, standing, hands upraised, hands shooting upwards in rhythmic gestures. 'Aye! Aye! Aye!'

Then the shouting died down, heads were bowed, and Angus signalled that all should sit.

He turned to Mungo and asked him to make clear to his friend Fittick what he was about to say.

'Our gods are those who care for us. Our gods are those who help us in times of trouble. Cailleach is our great mother, a healer and helps during childbirth. She is a creator, gentle and fierce, and a nurturing goddess.' He paused to see that Mungo had translated, then continued, 'Beira is our Queen and goddess of winter, who can raise storms and torrents, and we have to bow to her and make offerings to keep the peace.'

Fittick nodded.

‘I understand.’ He turned to Mungo. ‘There are no men here?’

Mungo smiled.

‘Wait!’

Finn stood again and face uplifted, roared into the skies.

‘Aengus, son of Beira, god of youth, hear us. Ogma, god of learning and speech, hear us.’

He paused, and made a wide circle with his arms, inclusive of everyone present.

‘We await you, we await your coming and invoke your help. ANAM CARA!’

Finn stood for a moment, lighted and warmed by the sunshine, face smiling as he stared upwards, hands upraised. Then he lowered his hands, lowered his head and stood again in repose. The silence was almost palpable. If he moved, Fittick felt the fragility in the air would be shattered. He remained as still as the others, scarcely breathing.

Finn sat down, and everyone eased, moved, stretched, patted the shoulders of their neighbours, smiled to each other. The mood had changed, lightened from solemn entreaties to friendship and harmony. Then Finn turned to Fittick.

'Now my friend, we hear you!'

Fittick was ready. He too had been stimulated by Finn's performance. He had felt included, and also entranced by the music. But his calling was strong. He stood tall, hands upraised.

'In the name of the Father, the Son and the Holy Spirit,' he called. 'I come to you to tell you of our Lord, Jesus Christ, and God, His Father, and our Father. God and Christ are for us all, and all within us. There are no separations into parts, like water, like health. Christ is Whole.'

He began with the story of Mary and the angel Gabriel's appearance. He described the journey of Mary and Joseph and their begging for a place to stay. He told of the manger. And he continued with the Star of Bethlehem and the journey of the Three Wise Men.

The audience listened avidly. They loved stories and Fittick was excelling himself as a storyteller. His belief, his certainty and his excitement at the birth of Christ was as compelling as was Finn's calling on their familiar gods.

Fittick paused at the birth, and the coming of the Three Wise Men.

'There is much more, much, much, more to tell you,'

he said. 'This is only the beginning. There are the miracles which Christ performed, there is the story of the boy Jesus in the temple where He said I must be about My Father's business. There are stories of Him as a fisherman with his followers. At the Sea of Galilee, He found Simon, called Peter, and his brother, Andrew, both fishermen, who were casting a net into the waters, just as you do. Jesus told them that in doing so they were to become "fishers of men", and to follow Him. Our gospels, books written by holy men called Matthew and Mark, tell these stories. And there is more, much more which I can tell you.

'But,' and he paused, and looked round his attentive audience. Not one had left the Circle. All were still, and intently focussed on him and his words. He continued. 'But what I want to tell you, most important of all, is about our knowledge of this Christ. Christ loved us and gave his life for us. He was crucified and died. He was buried. And on the third day He rose from the dead to show us there is life beyond death. He is seated now with God the Father Almighty, and He is for everyone, for all our needs and wants, for our goodness and to forgive our sins, to heal our souls. That is the God and Christ of my beliefs.

'The Good News I bring you is that Christ rose from the dead! He is Love, as God is Love. God so loved the world that He gave us His Son to die for us! And to rise again from the dead! He showed himself to his followers, to his mother and to others. He rose from the dead. As we will too if we follow Him. And we may show Him to your gods, too. Can we make a friendship with each other? Growing together in our difference as do the different plants on the hillside? Remember, He is Love!'

Mungo finished the translation as Fittick stopped, and bowed his head, crucifix in his hands.

Angus came to him, bowed and touched the crucifix. Seonaid walked up to him, and kissed the crucifix. Others followed.

Fittick stood, amazed. What was happening?

More followed. The company broke up, with the women chatting, excited – one God, only one. That could include all our gods. Some of the men were talking of the new God, they sounded excited. Worship only one God, with all our gods as part of Him? One God overall. But there were cautionary phrases.

'We need to hear more.'

'A fisherman? I'm interested but I want to know more.'

And,

‘I’m not so sure about this Christ mannie.’

And also,

‘This is what they’ve learned in Aberdeen, remember?’ One or two of the older men and women reminded the rest of Machar in Aberdeen, and back to Columba and Colman, active up in the north years ago. As far as Fittick could hear and see, some at least of the men and women were excited, enthusiastic about a new idea.

But there was one small group, perhaps five or six younger men, and some women with them, surrounding Finn. They were staring, and not coming forward. And they were scowling and muttering amongst themselves.

CHAPTER TWELVE

Angus turned to Fittick.

'Go for a walk, sir, while we discuss.'

'I wish to go with him.' Mungo sounded slightly defiant. Angus nodded agreement

'It is well. We are aware of your opinions, boy, and will keep them in mind. Go with your friend.'

Reluctantly Fittick and Mungo moved out from the gathering, and set off down the stony path from the Circle. The sky was blue with fleecy clouds, the waves were a gentle whispering sound on the shore.

'Shall we go to the Well?' Fittick suggested. 'Beside the water which will shine on all of us – Christian and local gods together.'

The slow-paced walk between the shore and the start of the hillside, from the human places to the sparkling water, was balm to the grinding anxieties in both Fittick and Mungo. The words 'what if' hovered on their tongues and they looked at each other occasionally, wanting to ask, but fearful.

Fittick had enjoyed the slow pace, listening to the eternal sound of the waves splashing on the shore as they moved across the shoreline. He enjoyed the crisp crunch underfoot of the shingle and small stones, and stumbled from time to time on the larger stones. Keep watch, he adjured himself. Keep a look out! The shore was still free from its usual human activity, but some gulls were pecking busily on the shingle. There were no women down there collecting and carrying seawrack back to the settlement, no men tending the boats and oars, no women mending the nets. A quiet day indeed, with everyone round the Circle, a strong community sharing ideas and wishes. And only he and Mungo were absent.

Eventually Fittick said, as they neared the Well,

'So, Mungo my friend, what if they turn me out? Where can I go?'

The words broke the spell of the walk.

'It seems to me,' Mungo was still considering the doings in the Circle, 'that there is a lot in common in our different worship. Gods who care for us, gods whom we can ask for help, gods who will help us. And the Christian God likewise.'

'I felt very privileged to attend, and to be asked to speak.'

Mungo laughed.

'You sound exactly like some visiting head man, someone hoping to please the right people. Very prim and proper.' He meant, not like yourself at all Fittick. Not like the enthusiastic young man he was beginning to know. He laughed again. 'Anyway, they wanted to hear from you, Fittick. They didn't want to ignore you or be hostile …' Mungo's voice trailed off. There had been a hint of hostility. Some of the Circle members had looked aggressive. Bravely he tried to finish on a positive note. 'They needed to know more – and you gave them that.'

At Mungo's words, Fittick looked back. Angus and Finn were in the centre of the Circle, Finn gesticulating as he talked. A man whose wife and daughter said he was unwell. A man who had showed considerable enmity. People seemed to be gathering around him, listening - he was the big noise in the discussion.

Fittick bowed his head, made the sign of the Cross on his chest and returned his crucifix to its usual place under his shirt. Eagerness rose in him.

'I shall say some prayers at the Well, and ask for blessings on it again.'

Mungo was uneasy.

‘Shouldn’t you wait for permissions from the elders, Fittick?’

‘Surely not! It is a public place, of a certainty. One in the open air! Are not all able to visit this Well as we wish and need?’

‘I agree, but …’ Mungo’s voice trailed off. He knew, better than Fittick, the anger of some at the introduction of the Christian God, although why they were so angry bewildered him. After all, it could do no harm, he argued. Prayers at the Well, even to an unknown God, were valuable. Surely! And so he would argue if he needed to. And he might need to, he thought, as he heard shouts from men striding towards them.

He and Fittick reached the Well and Fittick stood on the small platform below the water. He gazed up at the water, sparkling as it rose from the earth, making an arc as it fell. Its beauty and clarity seemed to him to signal great goodness. Then he bent his head, and traced the sign of the cross on his chest, ready to begin his prayers.

‘STOP!’

Finn was leading a small band of younger men, followed by Eilie, and Seonaid with small Alys in her arms. He reached the Well and stood just below Fittick on the platform, drops of water splashing on his grizzled head.

'What is it that you have just done, man?' snapped Finn. 'We saw you. What was that about?' He clenched his fists. 'You are in our settlement. You obey our rules!'

The transcendence of the moment was shattered. Stunned, Fittick turned to stare at him and his followers. The feelings of interest and sympathy from the Circle meeting were wrecked. Finn had not been persuaded into understanding nor into friendship. He was still angry.

Fittick stammered,

'I am but saying a prayer, sir, in thanks for the healing properties of this Well.'

Finn spluttered.

'And our gods? Do they mean nothing to you? After what you have heard us say in the Circle?'

'Indeed, I think they may come to mean much. If we introduced Christ Jesus to your people, and you introduce your deities to me, we will have a friendship.'

Fittick tried to explain his ideas again, carefully, still forcing himself not to sweep aside the pagan deities to be replaced by the One True God. From all he had been taught, the Christian God was supreme. He must triumph. It must happen – but slowly and gently, he thought.

But Finn shouted,

'You are not welcome here. You will leave!'

Angus arrived, slowly, holding his staff as a prop to help him across stony ground and up the hillside.

'WAIT, Finn! Wait, elders!' shouted Angus. 'This man has done no harm!'

Finn roared back.

'He should have waited for us! He has prayed over the Well again! He should have requested our permission!'

Angus nodded.

'True, he should! But he is as faithful to his God as we are to ours! And he wishes to set his God here along with ours.'

Another elder stood by Angus.

'He has not set his God against ours, remember! He wishes a friendship.'

There was a rumble of agreement round the ring of men.

‘Aye, that’s the way of it.’

‘That’s right.’

‘That’s so.’

Most of the comments were friendly and kind. But there were others.

‘We don’t need more gods.’

‘Why have a Christian God when we have plenty here?’

‘It will soon be the Winter Season and we will see or hear our goddess Cailleach.’

‘Cailleach will not be pleased to have another God near her.’

And again,

‘We need no more gods!’

Finn raised his voice again, fists at the ready.

‘He is wearing you down! He will divide us. Some will believe him. Some will not. But we must be loyal - to each other! And to our gods! They have been good to us. And to our fishing! He will split us in two. And we need to be together! He will split husbands from wives!’ Finn was howling now, and he thrust his fists into the air, demented. ‘He is a stranger. He must wait! And bide away from the shore.'

Again there was a rumble of agreement, as some nodded at the comment.

Eilie came up and stood in front of her husband.

'Nothing will split us, Finn! You know that! But look!' She turned to the assembly. 'And look again!' She took Alys from Seonaid's arms. Now she put the child on the ground. Alys stood straight and slowly took one step, then another, then another. Eilie said, 'This has been done to Alys, this healing. And it came after Fittick had been with her. So take care, Finn!'

'He will not split you from me!' Finn backed off, but the anger remained in his face, though now mixed with some doubt. 'But I say he should leave us.'

Another elder came puffing up to where Fittick and Mungo stood.

'I fear what Finn says is correct. I feel for you and for your God, and many of us understand and we want to know more of this new religion. After all, even the monks up the coast at Portmahomack told my people much of Christianity. And there was Machar in Aberdeen and the great Columba. These men were good men, and their followers are good also. This new knowledge is slowly coming to all of us. But to do so will take time.'

Angus nodded his own agreement.

'Go slow, go slow. Indeed, it will take time. And we fishermen understand a slow and steady pace.'

Fittick bowed his head.

'I understand, and I will go slow. But the urge came upon me when I arrived at this Well. And I believe it came from my Lord and Master, Jesus Christ, whom I have sworn to obey.' Before he could stop himself, he raised his head and roared, 'We are all one! We can be united as friends, our gods and us!'

'Ach, Fittick, pipe down!' Mungo snapped. 'You're just goading them on to fight, man, do you not see?'

He was right. The band surrounding Finn started forward, two men at the head, their fists at the ready. Finn shouted again.

'Take care!' and the men began to sidle forward, menacingly. Fittick stood transfixed on the narrow platform below the water, horrified at what he had called into being. He felt like kicking himself. Once more he'd opened his mouth when he should have kept it shut. This was one of his sins, the Bishop had told him. Had Angus not said too? Go slow, go steady. But he had pressed on too fast.

A new note sounded. Alys shrieked.

'Mama, Nana, Aunty Sho. Bad, bad, bad!'

'The child is right! This is bad! Finn, step back.' Eilie pulled at his sleeve. 'Think of the child, kin to you. Do you want her to see fights? Grow up with anger?'

A couple of the men pulled back, but the others continued to stand round Fittick and Mungo. There was nowhere they could go. Sideways, into a couple of angry young men. Forwards, Fittick would have met head-on with Finn in his anger. Backwards, into the Well itself. The two men stood and waited, tense and watchful.

Angus pushed his way through.

'That's enough of that! That was not well done, Fittick! You are subject to our rules here! Remember that! And take it quietly!' He turned to Mungo. 'Mungo, take the man up the hill towards Alasdair's broch, and you know there are some small dwellings built up there. Wrecks maybe, but something could be made of one of them. Get him out of here at any rate.'

The aggressors pulled back, pleased that Angus had reproached Fittick angrily, sure their headman was on their side at last, sure now that Fittick would leave. They rejoined the group, their eyes turned kindly to Alys and on Eilie. They had known Alys's mother and father, and sympathised. They would all take part in helping the difficulties of a family deprived of two of its members, and with Finn growing older. The women would share vegetables and herbs if Eilie and Seonaid needed. If Eilie was sick, then Seonaid would look after her. And they were all there ready to help in whatever way they could. This seemed more important to them than whether Finn shouted the name of Cailleach and Fittick the name of Christ! The details were important – yes, the gods were there to help, but … the practicalities of care were to the living.

But Finn was still pushing for a fight. He still stood in front of Fittick. Mungo stepped down from the platform to Finn's side, and one or two of the older men edged forward. One of them took Finn by the shoulder.

'Na, na, na, lad. We can let him go peacefully.'

Eilie came alongside again too, and clung to Finn's sleeve.

'Please, Finn, for the sake of the bairnie.'

Finn subsided. Eilie had got through to him at last.

Angus, still close to Fittick, murmured,

'Take care, Fittick. There are some who do not wish

you well. And it might have been best if you had waited before blessing the Well again. And before giving us your message of unity.'

Fittick did not agree. He had not been aware of the following of the crowd, and he felt the moment for such a prayer had been a good one. But he did regret his cry for unity. He needed to watch his tongue, he reminded himself. He tried to say as much to Angus, but the chief elder was busy now.

'Mungo, it would be well to house him away from the shore, away from Finn and his family. Take him further inland as I have suggested.'

'Yes, Angus, I shall do so.' But as they moved from the Well, inland towards the route leading to the old village of Torry, Finn followed them, brandishing a stick.

'Go carefully! Or it will be the worse for you.'

CHAPTER THIRTEEN

Fittick turned to Mungo, his translator and, he hoped, still his friend. Mungo was shaking his head.

'You must leave here. You must depart. Angus, our chief elder, has spoken.'

'To where?'

'Angus has suggested a place near Alasdair's houses. We must take a look. We must think.'

'Perhaps it is best I become a hermit. Then people might come to me of their own free will. And I shall avoid the angry ones.'

Mungo looked bewildered.

'A hermit? That is, one on his own. Completely alone. But still in this place?'

'It is possible,' said Fittick. 'If I may find a place to live, away from these people. Perhaps on the hillside? Perhaps further?'

Mungo was nodding.

'Yes, yes, I see what you mean. A small place of your own. Which you will tend. You will make your own hearth, your own food.'

Fittick supplemented these ideas with,

'I will also have my own prayers, and my own worship. I shall have Christ Jesus depicted on my doorway, to be seen by any who might enter. And Christ on my wall, to be a reminder of the good life.'

'Let us find such a place.' And Mungo strode off, shouting over his shoulder. 'I shall ask. Wait here! I shall ask Alasdair and his elders.'

Fittick looked wearily back at the Well.

'I may be near you, I do hope and pray,' he muttered.

He remained, praying by the Well as he silently waited for Mungo's return. Mungo was not long in coming back. He looked pleased.

'I have found the very thing!' he announced triumphantly. 'Look up there!' And he pointed, behind Fittick, to a turn in the hillside. 'Behind that slope is an old dwelling. It needs tidying and mending. But that we can do. And there,' he paused, unsure of Fittick's reaction, 'you may be at peace, by yourself, and in very truth a hermit. And,' he added, 'you are far enough along the hillside from the lepers.'

'At the same time,' added Fittick 'I may be available to any who wish to know more about my Lord and Master, Jesus Christ, and God, the Father.'

Mungo groaned at the continued emphasis.

'I expect that can be arranged.' He turned, brushing aside some sage and yarrow that was growing by the Well, his irritation still obvious. 'Come, let us investigate.'

The hut proved to be all that Mungo had described. It was derelict, sagging walls, openings, crevices, broken roof. But it was peaceful, in a setting of wildflowers, the healing yarrow and sage, chamomile, daisies, buttercups and no doubt, dandelions. The hut was not within sight of any other dwelling in the area, not even the huts on the opposite hillside. It had great possibilities, Fittick thought. His mind had been dwelling on the first laying of stones to construct a small chapel. But let the house be mended, first. So let it be, he thought. If he was meant to come here, Christ would support him. But he would need help if it was to be made habitable. Brought up, as he was, in a family who always had hired help, he was completely incapable of mending anything. He looked helplessly at Mungo, eyebrows raised.

Mungo was talking fast.

‘I can help, and I know of others who will help, and by the end of the day, this hut will be sufficiently warm and secure for you to sleep in.’ He looked round and pointed to a small wooded area further up the hillside. ‘Go you and gather sticks for a fire, and small stones to make a hearth circle. Whilst I will go and get my friends to help mend this structure.’

Mungo was right, and, with his friends helping, by early evening, the stone and wood hut walls were secure, with holes mended and a wooden door swinging to close. Fittick had only managed to make a hearth and build up a pile of firewood. However, he had acted as runner between Mungo and his friends, fetching and carrying wood and stones as required.

At last Mungo stretched out for the roof. He climbed on the shoulders of one man, while the other passed up wads of heather which Mungo stuffed into the holes in the roof which he could not yet mend with wood or stone. He jumped down from his friend’s shoulders.

‘There!’ he gasped. ‘That will do nicely in the meantime. It will require more, but for the nonce …’ He turned to Fittick. ‘We will go now, sir priest, ... uhm ... friend Fittick. May you be warm and comfortable tonight.’

'Bless you for what you have given this day. Thank you!' Fittick made the Sign of the Cross. The home-menders turned with a grin and a wave to go back to their own places.

'I shall be off soon, too, Fittick, my friend. But I shall make sure you have what you need.' Mungo was checking the firewood stack and adding to it, from the small pieces of branches he could find on the ground.

With mixed feelings, Fittick turned to his new home. He felt alone. Mungo would be soon gone. But he felt also exhilarated. This was his chance now, to become the missioner he wanted, to serve Christ, to live the gospels as best he could.

Stones sliding behind him made both them turn. Seonaid stood there, pot in one hand, bannocks in the other. She was alone.

'I had not seen you climb the hill!' Fittick exclaimed.

'I have made you a broth, and brought some bannocks, good sir,' she said. 'For you will not have had time to gather food for yourself.'

She looked at the small house.

'I may enter?' she requested. And on receiving Fittick's nod of permission, she moved in with her pot to place it on the hearth which he had created, but not yet lit. He followed her inside, watching. Mungo and his friend were finishing the firewood stack outside.

She rubbed two sticks together until she got some sparks, making them fall on to the dry stems and bits of wood on the hearth. And gradually as the sticks caught fire, the wood began to crackle, and the flames came through. Seonaid reached forward and placed the pot in the centre. 'Now it will do nicely,' she said. 'And Eilie will bring you some porridge in the morning.' She rose from her knees, dusted down her skirts and smiled. 'I must go and tend the bairn now. May the hut bring you warmth and safety.'

Fittick took her hand in thanks. But her reaction was unexpected. She clutched his hand in both of hers. He tried to pull his hand free, but her grip tightened, and she moved closer to him. He gazed down on her shining hair and deep brown eyes. Her mouth held the hint of a smile, and her eyes were inviting.

He bent his head, his mouth met hers and they kissed, a warm, loving, inviting embrace, his arms holding her tightly. She put her arms round his neck and nuzzled against his shoulder. He had a sudden vision of what marriage to her would be like, the body, the spirit, the utter enchantment of such a woman.

But the pressure of the crucifix on his chest stopped his thoughts, reminding him of his promises, of the

One whom he desired to serve, above all others. The pain in his heart mirrored that of the ache of the crucifix on his breast. He stepped back swiftly, as she stared at him in perplexity. She made a move towards him again, and he raised his hand to stop her.

'This must not be, my love, oh my dear love! This cannot be!' His emotions made him hoarse, but the words were clear.

'Surely, you do not have to be a man by yourself?' She must have learned only very recently the ways of his church. He shook his head.

'It is so with me!' The firmness in his voice made her step back, step away, move towards the door, her face downcast.

He held his hand high in blessing. No woman, and certainly not this woman, was for him, he reminded himself. However, it was hard to ignore the warmth and tingling and movements within his body. Had he made the right decision? Was it really his calling to be a celibate?

'May you be happy in your new home.' She stumbled over the words, as Mungo and his friend walked back up towards them. 'I must go home.'

'We too will go to be with our families,' said Mungo. 'I shall return tomorrow to ensure all is well.'

Had Mungo seen him kissing Seonaid? Was this the usual behaviour of young women in this part of the world? He thought probably not, his mind in a swirl of confusion, with pleasurable memories, but with anguish at betraying a trust – to Mungo, to his own calling, and to Christ.

As he watched, hand upraised in farewell and mouth forced into a smile, Seonaid with the two young men left to walk swiftly down the hillside to their warm, friendly, family homes.

Fittick felt more alone than ever before. With no friend, and maybe worse, no Seonaid, he was in a vast landscape, with the sea shushing on the sandy shore, with the wind siffling through the trees and raising the leafy plants to move gently in the breeze. And the dusk was falling, with no friendly light beside him, or even in the distance. And his anguished memories for companionship.

He was alone!

But even as he felt the silence heavy around him, he thought,

'This is what I wanted. Now I must bless the place to Christ's use and His ministry. I am not alone while He is with me.'

Fittick turned, raised his crucifix towards the hut

door, and spoke words of blessing on the hut, praying that Christ would use it for His ministry, and bring people to hear His words.

No longer burdened with feelings of solitude and the heavy silence it can bring, he entered his new home, light of heart, savouring the tangy scents of the stew simmering on the hearth. He knelt to feed more sticks into the fire. His own fire, his own hearth. And his Master for care and company.

CHAPTER FOURTEEN

He prayed long that night. And maybe his prayers helped him sleep. Give to God and Christ the failures, the aggression, being turned away, quarrels with new friends. Give to God and Christ his feeling of Seonaid's body against his, and the conflicting longings for her with his longing for Christ. He prayed,

'Christ, if it be Your will, take this burden from me. And guide me.'

And he slept.

An early wakening with a clear mind proved to him that Christ had listened to his prayers. With thanks in his heart, he said his Daily Office and some extra prayers for the benefit of his new home and his friends, and for others to become his friends. And a thought took him outside the door. He looked across at the hillside where the lepers' huts were built. He raised his crucifix in their direction and called a blessing.

Then he strolled round his small dwelling. Explore! he thought. Move round the hillside. Move up. Up and beyond. Go seek! Up towards the lepers' dwellings. Maybe the time was coming to include them in his daily Christian worship. Greet and keep a distance. And offer prayers.

As he strode he became aware of the clouds gathering above the waters and the sea moving with slow, tremendous waves. He could see small boats battling, and raised his hand in blessing. They must be the smaller fishing boats, he mused, out for the day's catch. What is it they catch so near to shore? Herring, he knew, were further out to sea. He was no fisherman, Fittick! Although he was keen to learn. And like most people, he loved the flavour of fresh caught, fresh cooked fish.

A shout made him pause. Mungo was climbing the slope fast.

'You are not with the boats, then?' asked Fittick.

'No, I shall go out later or tomorrow. Depends on the tides. Today I want to make sure you have all you need. And …' Was there a hesitation in the voice? 'Maybe we can have a few people come up here later today for you to tell us a little more of your Lord and Master, the Christ?' The question was indeed hesitant, and Fittick was swift to agree and change the hesitancy to certainty.

'Indeed, yes, gladly, I shall do as you wish. If … your friends are happy to do so?'

It was his turn to be hesitant and questioning. Mungo nodded.

'Oh, indeed they are. These are the ones who have learned something from the community at Portmahomack in the North, who have learned from Colman, and who have travelled far and wide and met with this new thinking.'

'What is it that attracts you and your friends?'

Mungo stopped in his climb to think, head down, frowning.

'Methinks it is the love – it is – how shall I say it? It is general, for all, it is not one person for one thing, such as a goddess for birth, a god for hunting. It is a, a big feeling, stretching forth to all.'

Fittick beamed his joy.

'Indeed, my friend, that is what it is. We forgive our enemies, we love those that despitefully use us and we give to those in need. And there is more.'

Mungo grinned happily.

'We will learn of you all you can teach us.'

They finished their climb, reaching the top of the hill,

and paused.

'Over there,' and Mungo pointed, 'is the village of Torry. A small place with fine people, fine sailors and women who can gut a fish in seconds. And they too have learned from Colman and from Machar from his time in Aberdeen, the place beyond Torry.'

'Tell me more.'

'Torry is one of the greatest settlements of fishers I have ever seen,' declared Mungo. 'Though there are few people there, every wee family is involved with the fishing. The men go on the boats, sometimes any boat that's needing a fisherman or two. While the women and bairnies ...' He paused.

'Go on,' prompted Fittick. He was intrigued by this different way of living, so unlike his own farming and land-owning background. 'What do the women do? The same as here?'

'Aye, they make nets, they mend nets, they take the fish from the boats, and they have taken on our special way of smoking them, and it is delicious!' Mungo smacked his lips. 'If anyone offers you smoked herring from Torry … grab it at once!'

Fittick laughed.

'Indeed, you have told me that some of these ideas came from your own travels. Go on! Anything more?'

'Bairnies play round the place, the houses are small, but cosy, and aye, I'd like fine to have a wee house in Torry, even if it meant leaving Ma and Pa here.' Mungo reverted to the local dialect.

'What about their beliefs?' Fittick did not forget his own wishes. 'You said that some of them follow Columba and Machar?'

'Aye, maybe you've heard the story. God told Machar to make a church where the river bends into the shape of a bishop's crozier.'

'And that's where?' Fittick was impatient for the story.

'Just in Aulton, the oldest part of Aberdeen, where the River Don bends just like that. And that is where Machar was told to build his kirk, and where he preached to the folk there.'

There was a lot left out, Fittick thought. How did Machar find the river, who did he preach to, were there arguments? But no doubt he could find out, slowly. The first thing was to deal with his own situation.

But at least he was not alone in his mission, reflected Fittick. Indeed, others, greater than he, like Columba, and Machar, had been before him. He would build on their work, and learn as much as he could of what they had taught.

They turned on the brow of the hill and looked down towards the settlements and the sea, now dotted with small boats inshore, and with bigger boats further out. Then they looked along the hilltops to where the lepers had built their huts.

'I need to learn more about the fishing,' Fittick observed.

'Aye, but priests are often considered unlucky. You'd best not go on a boat or near a boat.'

'Our Blessed Lord was a fisherman,' Fittick reminded him. 'As were his disciples. All good fishermen.'

'That's so,' Mungo nodded.

'And as well,' Fittick continued, 'Brendan, the great Christian teacher of Clonfert in Ireland, he was a great seafarer.'

'But maybe no' a fisherman?' asked Mungo.

Fittick shook his head.

'I'd be surprised if he didn't fish, but no, maybe he didn't sail with the fishermen.'

'Best you just keep away, and bide on the land,'

Mungo suggested.

Fittick laughed.

'I must go and call a blessing to the lepers,' he observed. Mungo waved him off and began to run back down to his own dwelling and daily work. Fittick, meanwhile, turned across the hillside towards the lepers' dwellings, barely seen within the heavy fenced surroundings. Nearby, along the path, were woven leafy baskets, and pots heavy with food. About six baskets in all, Fittick counted. And a couple of flasks or so of ale, maybe, he thought. Water they could no doubt get for themselves, but ale might be harder to come by. Were these the flasks which Mungo had filled up the other night on their walk?

He looked down at the grassy slopes. Someone had dug over a plot of land, and planted it with vegetables. Had that been the lepers themselves? Or the goodhearted fishermen trying to help?

He reached the fence and called out the greeting he had learned from Mungo. A door opened and a face looked out. A face lumpy and smudgy, almost hiding the eyes peering in his direction.

'What do you want?'

'To say a prayer to the risen Christ on your behalf.'

The door slammed shut. It was not opened again, no matter how loudly Fittick called. He gave up in the end, raised his crucifix and shouted his prayer for help.

In the afternoon it was as Mungo had organised. Six people, Seonaid and Anna, Angus's wife, Eithne, and Mungo and two of his friends, sat round the hearth, comfortable on the soft cushions which Seonaid had brought. Her friend had brought a flask and she passed it round for everyone to sip from. Seonaid was maybe slightly cooler towards him than before, but pleasant and friendly enough, Fittick thought. He had no wish for any sort of quarrel with her, though determined to avoid any closer links. But Mungo sat closer to Seonaid than to anyone else, and Fittick wondered if he could read anything into that. There was the occasional interchange between them, while Fittick spoke the gospel of The Lord and Mungo ensured clear understanding by an occasional translation from Irish into Scots Gaelic.

Fittick began again with the birth of Christ, then continued with His becoming a carpenter like His earthly father, Joseph, then on to being a fisherman. He told of the disciples, and the fishermen amongst them. And he told of the miracles of healing which Christ did, avoiding the story of Christ healing the leper. Maybe that's wrong, he thought to himself, but he was aware of the fears of the group and their hostility towards the lepers. That was something to be tackled later.

‘That will be enough for this time,’ he said. ‘I will leave the anger of the Romans, the trial by Pilate and the Crucifixion until another day. Sufficient it is to say that His Mission was one of love and caring, of healing and kindness.’

There were questions: how could this be? Tell us more about Mother Mary. What did forgiveness mean? Fittick answered as best he could, while saying,

‘I am only a man, and have learned only so much. What I know I will tell you. What I do not know, we will learn from others, I do hope and pray.’ He did not tell them of his visit to the lepers’ dwelling, but in his heart, he added them to his prayers.

‘I will end with my favourite prayer.’ He stood and spread out his hands in blessing.

Our Father who art in heaven,

hallowed be thy name,

thy Kingdom come,

thy will be done,

on earth as it is in heaven.

Give us this day our daily bread,

and forgive us our trespasses,
as we forgive those who trespass against us;
and lead us not into temptation,
but deliver us from evil.

Everyone seemed satisfied, and as they were moving off, Fittick heard mutterings of 'Aye! Deliver us from evil. A good thing!'

As the others left, Eilie and Seonaid and one or two of the other women poked around in a small piece of earth at the front of his dwelling. They dug into it with wooden tools, tossed over the ground, and carefully poked some plants in. Fittick was delighted.

'Thank you! This is beginning to feel home-like.'

'That's the idea!' laughed Eithne. 'You are at home now.'

And besides their gardening work, the women had produced, from some capacious slings on their shoulders, three bannocks and another flask. It was cold, but Seonaid told him to put the contents in his pot on the hearth and it would soon warm up. He did so, grateful for the attention, but again anxious that there was more warmth in her feelings than he wanted. Although part of his being wanted to return that warmth, the greater part reminded him of his devotion to his Master.

CHAPTER FIFTEEN

On this second night he expected to sleep well. The warmth, the food, and above all, the interested companions, gave him a feeling of security.

But instead, he slept fitfully. Part of his mind was still focussed on the two colonies of lepers and their suffering. He wanted to find out what help was being given and what he might be able to do. His dreams of the leper's face he had seen was interrupted by a vigorous wind howling round his dwelling, clattering loose stones. There was a wailing in the air, and thuds and scrapes round the dwelling's walls. He got up, groggily, and went to the door. When he opened it, all was still. He stared out, he walked round the front of his small dwelling, he peered at the sides and went to the back. No one there, nothing was there. But the noises had made him alert. These noises were human work, he thought. Made to frighten him. This was an outpouring of anger, but in secret. Hidden anger was worse than open anger, more frightening because it could not be faced. What was he to do?

He returned to his bed, again to lie down and try to

sleep. But sleep did not come. His senses were alert to every noise. But silence reigned.

Mungo did not arrive in the morning. He was out fishing, Fittick remembered. So Fittick could not consult him as to the night noises. He wondered whether he should continue exploring, or whether it was safer for his dwelling that he remained nearby. He looked round the outside again. There had been an attack on one wall, marking it with big slashes. And some wood had been gouged out of another wall, leaving an ugly mark, but no hole.

He was sure these marks had not been there before.

Outside in the garden which the four women, Eithne, Eilie, Anna and Seonaid had planted the day before, plants were pulled out and left lying on the surface. Earth had been kicked around and the rough wooden cross he had made, to signify the entrance to the garden and his dwelling, had been broken into several pieces.

He decided to remain by his hut, and replace the plants first, rather than visit the nearby lepers so early, as he had planned. Instead, he set to to carve the figure of Christ on the wooden door. Protection, maybe, with the risen Christ gazing over the bay. He looked around for stones to cut with. A couple of sharp-edged stones lay near the hut. Had they been the ones used in the attack? Used to make noise in the middle of the night? Sawing, thudding, hammering noises? He inspected them. It seemed to him that there were traces of wood, tiny splinters stuck round the sharp edges. He was sure these flints had been used to attack his dwelling.

Thoughtfully, he returned to his door and, after a moment's contemplation, he made a start on his special carving. He marked out the shape of a man, from top to bottom, using damp soil to trace the outlines. This was to be a big figure. Then he began to scrape the lines, curve for the head, leave room for a halo, work at the face.

He was absorbed in his work, carefully and gently working on the face of Christ as he remembered seeing it in so many paintings. It was important to do justice to this portrait, to ensure the beauty of the countenance, the beckoning of the gaze, maybe a warmth in the slight spreading of the lips. The risen Christ, in the Bay of Nigg. Fittick felt a surge of enthusiastic creativity as he smoothed the wood shavings from the doorway carving.

A hand fell on his shoulder, and he started in surprise, turning to see who had interrupted his work.

It was Finn! Fierce and glaring with eyes sparking with anger, and lips with spittle of wrath at the corners.

'You will hold no more meetings! Do you hear?'

'I do but as I am asked!' Fittick gasped, wrenching his shoulder from Finn's grip. 'Should you not be telling your family what you want from them?'

Finn reached forward again to grip Fittick, this time by both shoulders. Fittick was determined not to fight him, but this ferocity was too much. He slashed upwards with his arms and broke Finn's hold.

'Ho!' said Finn. 'A man of peace? No fighting? That's what they said.'

Fittick said as calmly as he could,

'I protect myself, Finn, I do not fight, I do not wish to fight. But you will not overcome me by violence.'

'Say you so?' Finn snarled and lashed out with his fist. Fittick was alert, however, and dodged, and Finn's fist went straight into the unyielding wood of the door. He roared in pain. Fittick moved away.

'I suggest you leave now, sir, and return to your own home. Leave me in peace. I was a stranger to your shores, and you have rescued me, fed me and welcomed me. Let it rest at that between us.'

'Never!' snarled Finn. 'Until you came I was to

become chief elder with the gods in my hold. Now … with your God, you want to overcome our gods, to overcome our people. To overcome *me*!'

Fittick stared. This was not a debate about godliness. It was a matter of power, wielded amongst the families. He had thought that Angus was chief elder. Now it seemed that Finn was such, or wanted to be so. Could this power struggle … could it be more easily settled, he wondered? He would ask Mungo, and maybe even, could Mungo himself tackle it as mediator?

Finn dropped his hands, to Fittick's astonishment. He was braced, ready for another attack. But none came.

'You have not heard the last of this!' Finn snapped, and turning strode back down the hillside - just as two women were coming up. One was Eilie, Fittick realised. Finn paused and seemed to be arguing. But the two women carried on climbing the path.

Fittick looked downhill in amazement. There was to be no fight. Instead, Finn had given way, more easily than expected. What next? wondered the Irishman. Was it the thought of Eilie which made him give way? Fittick knew she had the ability to calm him and redirect him, as he had seen when little Alys was upset.

A call from further down the hill made him turn

again. It was indeed Eilie who was puffing up the hill, with a friend beside her. They were carrying pots and, could it be, bannocks? Fittick hoped so. He was a young man and he loved his food.

Eilie reached the hut and paused. She waved a hand at Fittick's outline, smiling.

'Your God?' she asked.

'Christ, His Son,' replied Fittick. 'I do but try to reproduce an image.'

Eilie nodded.

'Well done!'

And she put her pot down on the step at the front door.

'I will exchange this for what Seonaid brought you yestreen.'

Her friend smiled and proffered her armful of bannocks.

'This will help you through the next day or two.' She was laughing, knowing full well his voracious appetite, observed by the women at the hearth in the big shore dwelling.

'I misdoubt that!' Fittick joined her laughter. 'They are so delicious that I eat them all fast.'

‘I will bring you more tomorrow,’ she promised. ‘And others are cooking for you, my friend, so you will not have to cook for yourself. My experience is wide, and I have yet to find a young man who can cook anything fit to eat.’

Eilie took the pot inside and deposited it by the hearth, and picked up Seonaid’s empty pot. Fittick protested,

‘I have not yet cleansed it!’

She laughed heartily and slapped him on the shoulder.

‘Give way, our friend, give way. We will see to the cleansing for you.’ But at the entrance she was sober as she left. ‘Good sir, be careful. Finn is a very angry man.’

‘Why so?

‘I cannot say. No, I cannot say.’ And Eilie left, with a wave of the hand.

CHAPTER SIXTEEN

Bemused by Eilie's last words, Fittick helped himself to some of her broth and slumped on to a stone seat just outside the door.

He slid his tongue along a small leaf, and lost Eilie's comments from his mind, in the glorious flavour. It tasted of lemon, something which he had loved in France. What was this leaf? He must ask about that. Among other things he needed to know. Like washing dishes, washing clothes, mending if necessary, getting better footwear. His sandals were nearly in bits and it was hard going on the shingle.

After the meal he wondered how best to cleanse the pot. He did not want to use water from the Blessed Well. Was there another nearby, maybe one that he'd missed on previous walks? He clutched a bucket in one hand, and set off on a path slanting off from the straight path he had taken the day before. He could get a different view of the hillside round its steep curves. A steady pace brought him up the steep path, stony and ridged. Halfway up he stopped and looked back. The blue of the sky was reflected in the calm sea with its gentle waves. Way out from the settlement on the shore he could see the small boats fishing. The settlement itself was busy, he could see women bending over nets, and some down on the shore's edge, collecting seaweed for smoking fish, as well as some delicate pieces for cooking and eating. The day was so clear he could even see the outline of the smoking frame. He pushed back his thick hair and grinned down at the unknowing people. He loved them, they had rescued him, and even though there were disagreements, he felt some kinship with them. How much that meant Seonaid he refused to consider.

Fittick turned back to the hillside and another short walk took him round the slope to face down towards the village of Torry. A small place, not many houses that he could see. Some had tiny gardens, other houses were simple huts. And not far away from the houses, there were boats hauled up on the shore. Women were moving around, they had baskets on their backs. Full of fish, he guessed, to exchange, to sell.

The richness of time was entrenched in his mind, at that moment. He at this moment, six centuries, many said, after Christ stood on the earth, was standing here in this foreign land to tell of Christ in Jerusalem hundreds of years ago. Time had not stood still: time had polished the message, the message of love from the Master, Lord Jesus Christ. Time and His followers had burnished it from the simple love and care of which Christ showed and spoke, to the lives and practice of hundreds or more of men and women, spreading the message even further. Regiments of men and women. With overlords, with followers, with agreements and disagreements. But the message had kept on throughout time.

And, also, he thought, throughout place. He was standing in this foreign land. And the message came from Jerusalem, from Bethlehem, via France, Ireland. The message had travelled far and wide. A worldwide message. Yes, he had known this before, known in the practical sense of preparations and travel. But now there seemed to be a deeper meaning, possessing his soul with a spirituality he had never known before.

He was rapt, feet firm on the hillside, eyes on the heavens.

Then he began to shiver. The sweat from his striding up the hill was cooling and beginning to chill him. But the shivering came too from recognising the magnitude of the message.

The practicality of returning back to his dwelling hit him. He had to return, and step by step, learn to live there. He felt he was living in two worlds. One world was the vision of the message, and the other was the practicalities of sharing this message. Sometimes slowly and sometimes fast, he had to work working on getting to know people and the place. This was the process, he thought, of translating the gospel message to those of a different set of beliefs. Step by step, bit by bit, day by day, maybe even hour by hour. That was his work! He laughed. Slowly does it, take care, he thought.

The hill path had been steep and bumpy, and the spiritual path would be the same. For the hill, he suspected it would be more difficult to walk down its rutted surface than it had been climbing up. He couldn't risk a fall! For the spiritual? Wait and see! The spiritual was close to the practical, he thought. The one would direct the other, and which would come first? Or would they take turns in directing, these two paths, the spiritual and the practical?

The practical was the immediate director. He needed to get downhill. And walking down that steep and stony path was a challenge.

Fittick looked around. Was there a better path? He couldn't see one, but he did find a big stick which he thought would act as a staff and hold him steady and balanced as he negotiated the ruts and ridges and the sandy slippery path back towards the shore. Slowly he trudged downhill, towards the small house he had been given. He had not found any stream whose waters he might use in cleansing his pots, nor even his clothes. He needed to ask.

Perhaps Mungo might visit later, and he could ask whether there was water for washing. In the meantime, he could use leaves to cleanse the pot, as he had seen his mother's servants do from time to time. Those in Ireland, anyway, before he had moved to France for his monastic training.

Back at his dwelling he sank down gratefully outside on a warm grassy bank facing down to Alasdair's settlement, and beyond to Angus's settlement. So he thought of them ... Sun warmed him and he closed his eyes. It had been a rough night, he remembered, with much interruption. But the walk had brought him through the mental turmoil.

He did not know for how long he had dozed. But a shout woke him and brought him to his feet. He stared at Mungo sleepily.

'You here, my friend? I thought you were fishing.'

'We had a good run, and I brought you a wee bittie.' Mungo produced a couple of fish from his basket. 'See, they're all boned and ready to cook over the fire. Can you manage that?'

Fittick grinned. True, he was no cook, but he thought

that even he could cook fish, as no doubt had his Master, over an open hearth.

'Question, Mungo, question, if you have time?'

Mungo nodded.

'First, where is the nearest source of ordinary water?'

'Oh!' Mungo laughed. 'Why, just over there, along the hillside.'

Fittick marked it, then went on to his next concern.

'What's wrong with Finn? He came to attack me, warn me off, told me, I think, that I'm getting in the way of …' he trailed off. 'He raised his fists. And I am ashamed, but I raised mine. In defence, believe me! And then Finn moved on fast.'

'Aye!' Mungo tugged at his chin, thoughtfully. 'He won't stand and fight. He makes the gestures, but ... if anyone was even to seem like hitting out at him, he would move away. It's that Finn wants to be chief elder, under our gods. He sees himself as the one who explains our gods to us, and us to our gods … to give us direction, in some way or other. But Eilie is not sure he should do this. And she says he has not been well. Not since their daughter Aisling was drowned.'

'I thought that might be it.' Fittick was thoughtful. 'Eilie and Seonaid have both mentioned he has not been well.' He got up and stretched. 'Come in, come in for a warm drink. You might need it after your fishing.'

And I have more need of some counsel, too, he thought, but he refrained from saying that.

Fittick stirred the embers, and the warm sage drink began to simmer. He took the pot off the embers and poured the liquid into two big beakers.

'Here. Good for you.'

Mungo sipped and emitted a sigh of pleasure.

'That goes down grateful,' he admitted. He sat on the broad stone, cross-legged, just outside the house. 'Not a bad wee place. Not bad. Did you sleep well?'

Fittick considered. Should he let Mungo know of his night-time visitor? On the whole, he thought, the more who knew, the more likely it was to stop.

'Well,' he began cautiously. 'At first, yes. But later … well, there were noises, and thuds and thumps as if someone was either trying to break something down outside or break in or …'

Mungo stared.

'Who would try and break in here?

Fittick laughed.

'Indeed. Nothing to steal. I thought, break in to break down, both dwelling and myself.'

'Frighten you off, like?'

'Something like that. But I will continue here, though: it would seem to be my mission.'

Mungo turned to the door and pointed at the carving.

'You have already begun, have you not?'

'To make our Lord's presence felt?'

'That's it!' Mungo got up. 'Well, I must be off. The boat needs some attention and I said I'd work at it.'

A thought slid into Fittick's mind - *and you will see Seonaid*, He was annoyed with himself. He'd resolved to put her out of his mind, now that he was no longer in the shore settlement.

A visit to the lepers would help. Now! He'd missed his morning visit thanks to his overnight visitors. But now he was determined to go, as Mungo waved goodbye.

Along the hillside he strode, praying as he walked,

'Lord of Hosts, help me understand myself and my feelings. And help me to help.'

He paused some distance from the fence. A shout to

the lepers made his presence known.

'Andrew! Nell! I have come to pray with you.'

Silence. Again, he shouted.

'Let me pray to our Lord for you.'

A sound! a voice! Someone was standing just behind the fence.

'Hello! Hello! I am Nell.'

He could just see her over the fence. And wished he hadn't. What could once have been an upright, beautiful woman was now a bent, white-haired old crone, with a face and hands smothered in the vicious disease.

'Thank you! Thank you for coming! My husband may join us, but yes, please, do pray. A prayer in which I can join.' Her voice was croaky.

'We will say the Lord's Prayer together.'

And in her own tongue of Scots Gaelic they prayed together, Fittick moderating his tone to accommodate her slower, quieter words.

Half-way through the prayer another voice joined in. Young, piping, and clear. The boy, thought Fittick. The son of the family. And another voice, the daughter too. Wonderful.

And another voice joined.

‘May we repeat this prayer, friend priest.’

Andrew! The man himself. Fittick was almost overwhelmed. To have them all join with him and to pray together. He held up his crucifix so they could see it.

‘Friends, we belong together through Christ Jesus. We are connected in prayer. May this continue!’

‘Amen!’ – four times over. Said by each one, and then repeated by himself.

He wept.

CHAPTER SEVENTEEN

Back at his dwelling, water fetched, he had not got far with his carving when another visitor shouted to him. He grinned to himself. What kind of hermit life was this? Visitors several times a day?

Angus joined him and pointed to the door carving.

'I admire, sir, I do admire.'

'It is of our Lord, Angus, who guards my door and myself.'

Angus nodded, and made a gesture with his hand which could have been the Sign of the Cross. He shook his cloak free.

'It is warm, is it not? Warmer than we often find at this time.'

Had Angus really come to talk of the weather? Fittick responded.

'What weather do you usually have now?'

'Cooler, much cooler. But …' Angus was gazing out towards the shore, to the settlement where he was headman, to the fishing boats way beyond in the distance. 'I have come … to ask a favour, possibly.' He turned back to Fittick. 'May we speak freely, Fittick?'

Fittick nodded and gestured to Angus to sit down. 'There is much I do not understand, Angus. I would be pleased to know more.'

Angus was a large man. The stone seat outside the house just held him as he settled down, easing his feet in his boots, pulling his cloak back to enjoy a closer warmth from the sun. Fittick had to squat beside him.

'There are things I can tell you, and of course, in confidence. That much is agreed?' He pulled at his beard, avoiding Fittick's gaze by staring at the shore in the distance. His discomfort was obvious and Fittick hurried to reassure him.

'Of course.'

'It is as you may have guessed, it is … I want to speak a little … of my kinsman, Finn. We were once so close, but now …' His words trailed off.

'What happened?' Fittick asked gently.

'I married Eithne, and Finn, he married Eilie, a good

woman, a good healer. But I suspect Finn wanted Eithne. I do not know for certain. I do know that he was very angry at the time of my marriage. I was first of the young men to marry. But then as a boy he was always angry, about so many things – not enough warmth, not enough fish, not enough – oh, of anything, or everything. Bad sea, bad sky, bad weather. Too much sun, too little sun. That sort of thing. He is a great carver, great stonemason, great artist, but a somewhat impatient fisherman.'

'And not happy,' Fittick suggested.

Angus shook his head.

'No, not happy.' He leant his chin on his clasped hands. 'He married Eilie. A fine woman. And they have ... had … two daughters. Seonaid whom you know, and Alys's mother, Aisling, who was washed overboard with her husband. There are no sons. And he was angry. Said they should not have gone out that day. Aisling should have stayed home. Her husband should not have taken her out with him.' Angus bowed his head. 'It was a great loss to all the family. Finn suffered greatly at Aisling's loss. He loved her dearly, and of course, he loves Alys, but he had hopes of a son.'

'Aisling was expecting another?' Fittick questioned. Angus nodded.

'Yes! But I was first to marry, have sons … have become head man here, and all that was what Finn wanted …' He seemed reluctant to emphasize his importance as leader. As the senior man, he could lead his community towards Christianity. But that almost certainly would provoke enmity from some. And harmony in a fishing community, sharing boats, sharing nets and equipment, and the results of catch, was essential.

Fittick nodded his understanding. Angus continued.

'The religious side is that Finn says he was called by Lugus, our warrior god, and Camulos our god of war. And a few of our hot-headed young men follow him.'

'The gods of warriors and of war,' said Fittick quietly. 'Not ones to be followed or worshipped. They encourage fighting. While our God ...' he paused, wondering if he could use the plural 'our'. Angus nodded.

'Yes, our God, He is one of peace, is He not?'

'Peace and unity,' said Fittick. 'Harmony, forgiveness and love.'

Angus nodded, pulling at his beard again. A habit of his when thoughtful, Fittick guessed. He got to his feet, stretching.

'A drink, Angus, some warm ale from Eilie and

Seonaid? To drink to our own friendship – for so I feel it to be.'

Angus flung his head back and laughed.

'Yes! A drink! To seal our friendship.' He rose and followed Fittick into the dwelling. 'Whence came you, sir? You did not say much about yourself in our Circle meeting.'

Fittick explained his journey, ending with,

'And I wonder how my lady mother fares. She would go back to Ireland.'

'You have no means of knowing?

'None at all! No message will come from her since she knows not where I am, nor will the Bishop know, since I was washed ashore. I might be reported missing, and that would upset my lady mother.'

'You have no other lady?' Angus probed.

Fittick laughed.

'No, no, not I! Who knows but that that may come in time. But for my youth, I wish it spent in the service of my Master, going hither and thither. And that does not make for a good marriage or family life.'

'True! True!' Angus agreed.

'But in my turn, Angus, I wish to know more about the settlements here, in particular the houses on the hillside yonder. I have visited them – oh yes, I remained outside!'

'Ahhh! You have found our small leper domain? A sad business, indeed a sad business.'

'Mungo has explained the situation to me, about the man and his family.'

Angus nodded.

'I may add a few bits and pieces to what Mungo has said. We all do our best for them.'

'Let us go outside again.' Fittick took his drink in his hand and led the way. Angus followed. 'Mungo has already given me some information on this family, these lepers nearby.'

'Aye,' Angus replied. 'A fine local family, fine fisherfolk, a bit of a farmer, and a fine wife and grand bairns. They came from the place called Aberdeen, as Mungo might have said. Oh aye. Andrew was a grand sailor, took out the big boats, and sailed far and wide. Last year he got a boat for himself, to take his family out with him. They went to Scandinavia across the wide waters. And there, it seems, they met folk with the disease.'

'Surely they must have got too close?' He'd asked

this of Mungo, who had nodded his agreement. Angus was of the same mind.

'Aye, that's the like of it. Meeting, being friendly, biding with folk. Anyway, they came back to Nigg.' Angus fingered his beard again. 'We went out to welcome them. But he waved us off. Told us to keep away. And when he landed the boat, even though we were far off, we could see.'

See the dreadful disease, Fittick thought, on a man's face and body, and his family's also. People you knew, friends, kinsfolk. People you'd fished with, played with, walked with – all the details of friendship surged through Fittick's brain. Belonging! You and they belonged together. But this has set you apart.

'We shouted to them to go up the hillside to those dwellings. The houses were in fairly good condition.'

'Did they go at once?'

'No. First of all he shouted to us.' Angus groaned. 'I remember it well.' Fittick willed him to go on. 'Aye, fine do I remember it. He shouted he was going to burn his boat. He wanted no part of the disease remaining down here.'

'So what happened?' Fittick was eager to know.

'We left some burning embers for them on the shore

and … and we walked off. They came and got them. And put all the embers on their boat. And it went up like a light. The flames, well, you could see them from Torry, I'm sure.'

'Then?'

'And then they trailed off to the dwellings on the hillside. Anna, Aidan's wife, my own wife, Eithne, and Eilie and some of the other women had taken up some food and drink and the means of making a fire. They left everything there in the rooms, deerskins, cushions, stuff to make mattress. I know not all that was done, but the women caused the houses to be furnished and that right quickly. The family have been there ever since last year, not coming out, not meeting with us – we shout over the fence which they built to keep us all out.'

So that was the full story. Fittick was pleased to know so much but could only imagine the feelings of the family, of their community, and of its keen care of the sufferers.

From below the hillside, from a crowd on the shore, came shouts.

'Camulos! Lugus! Camulos! Lugus!'

Angus got to his feet.

'You have the whole of the matter now, Fittick.

There are many of us willing to be with you, and to link our gods with the Christian God and His Son. But some will not – and I have heard that the Christian God will have no other gods.'

'Can the Christian God not have friends?' said Fittick. 'Can we not invite them as wise friends at our feast? We should not dismiss your gods as if they had never been, nor held any sway over us and in our hearts. To my mind, they show the different interests, mayhap the different aspects of our God.'

Angus nodded.

'Fittick, you speak words of friendship, of harmony and love and kindness. This must go on.'

He left on his downward way to the shore, while the cries of 'Camulos!' reached up still. When Angus reached the shore, Fittick saw him hesitate. Would he tackle the local god worshippers? Or turn away?

He turned away, striding back to his own hut. Fittick could just see the figure of Eithne meeting him outside, and he thought he could distinguish Seonaid walking through the settlement.

He sighed and turned back to his carving. Christ was a man of peace, and He brought the thought too that all humans were sinful, and needed mercy and intervention with an all-powerful, ever-living God.

And God lived in heaven, in the skies, far beyond the earth. Where were these local deities to be found? And what did they say of human souls? He found no answer.

It was delicate work, carving a picture on upright wood. He chipped carefully, gathering the fragments into a bundle for his fire. Waste nothing, he told himself. Every little counts. Every small chip is fuel for the fire. And so it is with words and deeds, he thought. Small actions, small words … a handshake, a nod, a yes! And instead of No and But. He must remember that.

He finished wiping down the carving, and stood back. Looks quite good, he thought. He smoothed and polished Christ's halo, and the Cross in His hand. My Lord and my God, he thought. May I be worthy of You and take Your words to these people that they may follow You.

CHAPTER EIGHTEEN

Yes, there was sorrow in this place, and anger, and the tragedy of the lepers nearby. Yet Fittick felt he was living in a special atmosphere, sent to him on his walk on the hillside. Could others see him in this aura of blessedness? He now felt completely at home and in the right place to deliver his ministry. And he was certain of success. The blessing he had experienced on his walks remained with him, and his mission felt more secure, his beliefs underlined and supported.

Feeding his warm hearth from the wood pile kept up by his visitors, he thought he might be guilty of the sins of complacency. And though he felt he was moving forward with some of the community, he had made little progress with the family of lepers, despite his regular visits.

Over the next few weeks people visited him, in twos and threes, to admire his carving work, and to listen to him explaining the gospels of Christ. True to his intentions, he always used positive words, And, Yes, Agree, Friendship, instead of No and But, though these came through occasionally. The people brought food and drink to him: he had no need of hunting, though he learned to cook his own fresh fish, carefully, over the hearth fire. His small domain took on the atmosphere of a home, with his chosen ornaments signifying his love of nature and the links with Christ and his fishermen apostles. Stones, shaped like fish, or rounded in smooth shapes showed his liking for natural objects. Plants scented the small room, and brightened its darkness. His crucifix had its own place, hung on a wall, and was adorned by flowers picked daily. And wood strips lay on the hearth, ready to be used as needed when the fire died down and only smouldering ashes were left to rekindle. Pots stood beside the hearth, usually refilled by Eilie and Seonaid, and, dear to his heart, was a small cloth doll, made by Seonaid, and offered him by Alys, as a thank you, she said, 'for making me feel better'. He had received that gift with tears in his eyes, but joy in his heart.

Gradually it seemed that he was building a small community, as more and more came to him. Not just from the shore village, but from the small settlements dotted round the hillsides, those in view of the shores and those behind the other hillocks, tucked into the small glens. Even a few from the village of Torry came to see him. His days were composed of talking and listening to small gatherings. And of small acts of kindness and healing. Listening to individuals, sympathising, offering nourishment, walking with some, visiting the sick and blessing them. He was also involved with taking food and drink up the hill to the lepers, where he daily prayed and blessed them in their dwelling. They came out of their house now to join in and to welcome him, waving over the fence, keeping their distance. And of course, also praying for healing and comfort for other sick and injured. His days were fully occupied and wherever he went he brought the Good News, so that gradually he was creating a goodly number of interested Christian sympathisers. Some, he was sure, would refuse to leave their Celtic gods behind, even though willing to accept the new God.

But Finn refused to come, nor did his followers do anything but avert their eyes when Fittick came down from his hillside. He had no further dealings with Finn, though he tried. Holding out a hand. Smiling. Nodding in greeting. Nothing worked. Finn was adamant. Nevertheless, Fittick continued to include Finn and his followers in his daily prayers.

Then one day Mungo appeared in the open doorway.

'Come man, you may be wanted. Hurry!' He grasped at Fittick's sleeve.

'What's happened?' panted Fittick as he ran beside Mungo.

'Just come on!' Mungo waved him onwards.

Fittick ran down the hill to the shore behind his friend, more sure-footed now than when he first came. The stones on the shore crunched underfoot. Seagulls were calling urgently, swooping low. The waves crashed on the shore. Fittick peered at the cloudy sky.

'Are you taking me back to Finn's house? I will not be welcome – we might even be attacked.'

'No! No! It will be all right,' Mungo gasped, pulling him onwards, sliding over the shingle. They reached the house and stopped, leaning against the wall to catch breath.

And Eilie came out of the door.

'Please, Fittick, our friend, come in. My husband is so sick, so very sick. We have tried everything.'

Seonaid appeared.

'Sir, Fittick, we know of your acts of kindness. And your prayers for the sick and injured. Please help us, even though my father has been against you, and your beliefs.'

Alys was playing by the door. She smiled at him and raised her doll to show him.

'I love her,' she told him. He smiled and patted her head.

'Fittick, please.' Seonaid's eyes no longer held the invitation, the allurement which had all but fractured his vows. She was Finn's daughter after all. 'Please come in.'

Fittick stepped inside the dark dwelling once more. He had not been back since Eilie had succeeded in her wish to shelter him and Mungo from the anger of her husband and his followers. It was warm as were other places here. It had comfort, it had repose. But it also had sickness. Finn lay on a mat beside the hearth, his breathing rasping, his mouth open, his body constantly twitching. Fittick knelt by him. The heat from the body almost burned his hand.

'How long has this been going on?'

'Perhaps nearly a week,' said Eilie. 'We have tried all we know, all remedies of herbs and potions, sage and yarrow, sorrel soup. Nothing works. We have made him spew. He is still sick.'

'You have not tried water from the Blessed Well?'

She nodded.

'Just a little. But he spat it out. He would not swallow it.'

Fittick turned to his friend.

'Go you, please, Mungo, and fetch some water from the Blessed Well. Speak to no one on your way back as you hold the flask in your hand.'

Mungo ran from the hut. Fittick, meanwhile, continued kneeling by Finn.

'Eilie, do I have your agreement to my prayers?' he asked. She nodded. He freed his crucifix from his collar, and held it above the sick man. He made the sign of the Cross with his other hand and began to pray.

'Oh Lord, God of our Salvation, hear our prayers for this your beloved son, Finn, and his family. Help him in his sickness. Help him in his recovery. We ask this in the name of your Son, our Lord Jesus Christ.'

Eilie and Seonaid said Amen. And there was a small sound from Alys who was watching intently.

Did Finn's eyes open? Fittick thought there was some movement, but could not be sure in the darkness.

'Please, is there another lamp which I can hold to see more of this?'

Seonaid brought over two more clay lamps and gave one into his free hand. And he repeated his prayer, over and over again.

Some of Finn's young men entered quietly and stood by the walls, watching. Fittick saw them, and momentarily hesitated. He was unsure of their motives. If he failed to help Finn, would they attack him?

Panting, Mungo hurtled into the doorway, striding to the bedside. He held out the flask and Fittick took it, raised his hand in blessing and, kneeling again, moistened a cloth and gently drew it along Fittick's lips. They opened slightly. He squeezed a drip between Finn's lips. His mouth opened wider and Fittick wetted the cloth, and dripped more water between Finn's lips.

Finn swallowed. And at a sign from Fittick, Eilie came forward and helped Mungo raise Finn's shoulders, so he was semi-upright. Fittick then dripped more water from the lip of the flask into the open mouth.

Eilie drew back, and her stillness, reflected in the family and other onlookers, was almost palpable. They watched as Fittick repeated the dosage, and as Mungo continued to hold on to Finn's shoulders, raising him off the bedding.

Slowly, very slowly, Finn turned his head, and opened his eyes. He mouthed something. Mungo bent to hear. Finn mouthed again.

‘What goes on?’

The young men looked at each other, amazement in their faces. They pointed and smiled, and raised their eyebrows in wonder. One of them murmured,

‘He seems better?’

Another nodded.

‘There is improvement in his face.’

Eilie and Seonaid came forward.

‘You’ve been so sick, so very sick.’

‘And Fittick has cured you!’ Seonaid burst forth. ‘Without him, who knows?’

Fittick hushed her.

‘He may not be ready for that knowing.’

But Finn turned his head again, more easily this time.

‘You? You here?’

Eilie broke in.

‘I asked him, my husband, I was desperate to help you.’ She broke down in tears.

Fittick nodded.

'I came to assist, if you wanted me.'

'And we did. Oh, indeed we did!' exclaimed Seonaid.

Finn stared at her. He was exhausted from the sickness, lying back on his cushions. But he managed to see Fittick, and his eyes were clear. There was no enmity in the gaze, no anger this time.

'Thank you. Thank you. My friend.'

Fittick was stunned by the change. The clear eyes were unlike Finn's eyes as Fittick had known them. The priest stepped back, moved past the young men, once so intimidating and aggressive, but now, they were all gazing at him with awe. He went outside, still holding the flask of Unspoken Water. He laid it down by the door and bent his head in prayer.

'Thank you, God, thank you, Christ. Thank You! Thank You! Thank You.'

He had not given way to enmity. He had aimed to build friendship. He was as steadfast of his purpose as he had been when he began this journey.

And it seemed to be succeeding.

CHAPTER NINETEEN

The feelings of deep satisfaction and relief accompanied Fittick back towards his hillside home. As he climbed to the hillside from the shingle he thought he saw flickering lights in the leper dwelling. And was that a couple of folk running down the distant hillside? Maybe they had been visiting the lepers, leaving them food, like.

A shout from Alasdair's settlement confirmed his ideas. There was more light than usual in those small houses. Could it be ... could it be maybe extra lamplight, or extra hearth fire to cook by? He hoped so, as he hurried faster up the hill past his dwelling, towards the leper house. Alasdair was behind him, panting as he ran and climbed.

'With you, friend priest, with you,' Alasdair assured him. A fit man, fitter than Fittick, but the dark and slippery grassy slopes on the hillside made them both stumble and grasp at each other for stability.

'Looks ... looks ... bad,' Alasdair gasped.

‘Too much? too much light, and ...’ Fittick paused for breath. ‘What a noise!’

The roar of flames grew louder as they neared the leper dwelling, and the flames grew taller.

More shouts from behind them signalled the appearance of young men, from both settlements.

‘Don’t let them out! They’re unclean!’

‘They’ll burn! For sure!’ someone else yelled.

‘Send them away!’

‘They have to go somewhere else. They’re unclean. Do we all want to perish?’

Fittick barely registered the words. His whole being was focussed on circling the fence, trying to break in, break through the poles. He was sure he heard screams above the noise of the fire. And was that a figure he could see at the further end of the buildings?

Alasdair was beside him, pushing with a long pole at the burning fence posts. There was a crackling and roaring, as the posts creaked and broke down in bits. And as the poles rotted down, flames burst through the gaps in the fence, and swirled upwards, smoke accompanying them, into the darkened night sky. Stars were still flickering above them, but all their attention was on the blazing earth.

'HELP! HELP!' Screams came from beyond the remaining fence posts. A burning figure came staggering around the corner of the dwelling. 'HELP!' The flames licked at the tunic as the figure sank to its knees, hands over hideous face, hair smouldering on the scalp and down over its shoulder.

Fittick grabbed at his cloak and pulled it over his head. He thrust his way through the flames, regardless of someone trying to pull him back. Flinging his cloak over the figure, he squatted, patting, slapping, and as the figure fell, even jumping on to the cloak, tramping it down, bending over the figure to squash the flames. Fearful that the slaps might push the flames back on to the body and make it burn even more, he pulled back, and tried to shake the cloak free and throw it on to the ground beside the figure. And then stamped on it, while pulling a garment off the writhing body. The flames died down, but he could not recognise the face for burns, and the disease.

Meanwhile Alasdair was trying to do the same thing for another burning figure. Fittick could hear him gasping, against screams from the burning figure on the ground.

Two of the young men were chasing the other lepers, while there was a major battle going on amongst the other boys.

'Let them die! Let them burn! Cleanse the place!'

Horror-struck, Fittick stared at the person on the ground, the thing on the ground, he thought, with the flames extinguished. As he watched, the writhing and wriggling small movements slowed and stopped, and the figure sank even lower on to the grass. Dead.

He wanted to pray, but the mighty whoosh of a huge flame caught his attention. He stared as it sprang upwards, and at the same time, the small buildings themselves cracked, crashed, and slammed to the ground. One body could be seen outstretched, with small flickering flames encompassing the torso as it crawled out. His legs ended ... Good God, where? thought Fittick. Where his feet had been were two blackened stumps. Another body was burning, staggering, falling and squirming to reach the outside, head sparkling with small flames, bigger flames engulfing the clothing.

But parts of the building were falling. Alasdair and Fittick raced towards it. They wanted to draw it out, pull gently, pick it up and take it somewhere safe. Alasdair stooped towards the arms.

'It's the lassie! Wee Nell.' He slapped the flames with his bare hands, harder and harder up the arms' length to the shoulders. Then he slid his hands under the shoulders, as Fittick himself trod down and slapped the burning clothing. Alasdair slid his hands under the hips and together they stepped on to the cooler grass and laid down their burden – beside her brother, motionless on the ground. She was silent now, without one scream.

'Is she still alive?'

'Methinks, yes, but only just.' Alasdair was kneeling beside the small figure with its burnt and ripped clothing, its blackened legs and arms. He passed his hand gently over the frizzled hair. There were no more flames.

Wee Nell moaned. And moaned. The sound was heartbreaking. Fittick and Alasdair unashamedly wiped their eyes.

Slowly, the fires seemed to be dying down. Lack of wood, thought Fittick, glancing briefly. The young men, at least the fighting ones, had pulled back, leaving only those who wanted to help.

Alas, thought Fittick, there is no help now on earth for two of them. It seemed as if the man and woman had died of their burns, if not of their leprosy. The girl and her brother were still whimpering. He bent over them, smoke filling his lungs from the clothes and their hair. Their faces were leprous, and also burnt.

Mungo appeared.

'Be better if they died, wouldn't it?'

Someone beside Mungo agreed.

'Leave them. Just leave them be. They'll fade out. If they live, what's for them?'

Fittick felt anger rising. Human beings! Left to die? No! Leprous indeed, and maybe a poor future. But there was life, and life had to be preserved and cared for. He had never felt less in charity with Mungo.

Angus was there too, wheezing and gasping.

'This is terrible! Terrible! What happened?'

The boy moved slightly.

'They threw in a firestick.' His voice was hoarse, words slow. 'They wanted to burn us.' His sister moaned beside him.

Angus and Fittick looked at him, and looked at each other.

''Tis possible,' said Angus softly. ''Tis quite possible.'

'But we belong here!' the boy's voice was croaky with smoke. 'Ma! Pa!' Tears welled in his swollen eyes. 'What have they done to us?' He slumped down again. Fittick stooped and covered him over with a cloak, handed over by a silent Mungo.

The fire was dying down, almost completely dead now, with the last embers of the lepers' huts crumbling into ashes.

'What to do?' asked Fittick helplessly.

'We'll make a cover for them. They canna come into our houses as yet. They are still lepers. And they're so badly hurt. We daren't move them.' Angus was firm. He turned to his silent followers.

'You and you … go you and get some covers and we'll put in some sticks and make a roof to keep them ... safe as possible. Aidan, get me some big sticks if you can find any that aren't burned. And ... Aidan, again, get Eilie up here, if you please.'

Eilie and some other women came hurrying, woollens over their night tunics, heads covered against the cool winds.

'What's to do? what goes on?'

'Help these youngsters. Both badly burned.'

Eilie bent over them.

'I canna touch them, but ...' Using twigs as tools, she pulled back the burned clothes, and with her hands encased in deerskins, she stroked their faces. The girl moaned.

‘Hurts! Fire! Fire! They’re throwing fire!’

Eilie looked at Angus, who nodded.

‘That’s what the boy said, too. Looks like we’ve got some nasties here.’

Fittick stirred. He had been stunned into silence, but now he was moving again. Standing at the head of the two youngsters, he raised a hand, bent his head, and prayed.

‘God help them, God and Christ help their pain. Help us help them. God, this we ask.’

With Eilie he stooped again, and pulled a blanket over the two youngsters.

‘Will they live?’ he asked softly.

‘Who knows?’

Swiftly shelters were erected over the two youngsters. They were unconscious, but moaning in pain. Angus took charge again.

‘Eilie, please stay here for the while, and I’ll send someone to relieve you of the watch in about an hour or so. Mungo, I need you to march with me to check on the young men.’

Eilie turned.

'Send Seonaid up, please, Angus, with the special lotions for burns, and flasks of water.'

He nodded.

'Angus, I will remain,' Fittick said. 'I might be of use.'

CHAPTER TWENTY

Next morning Fittick tended his home and garden. He had come home in the early dawn when he could see the path to tread back to his home, leaving Eilie and Seonaid and some of the other women sitting with the two remaining lepers.

All he could think of at the moment was the fire last night. It was deliberately started. It was a deliberate conscious effort to get rid of the lepers. But who had done it? First thoughts centred round the young men who'd been throwing stones. But maybe there was more to it. That was something he would have to leave to Angus as head man, and to the elders of the community.

He should focus on prayers for the dead, and maybe the dying. He had left Eilie in charge of caring for the two youngsters, but he doubted they could live. And he needed to think of confession, of forgiveness, of absolution. If such could be the case, if there was an acknowledgement of sin, if ... if ... if. Fittick wished fervently that he had the advice and support of some of his colleagues. He felt very much on his own. Prayers seemed to ascend into nothingness; he had no feeling now of the risen Christ's presence.

There was a call from the path up to his doorway. Fittick looked up. What now? he wondered. He took a deep breath and muttered a brief prayer for patience.

'Hoi! Hoi!' came the shout again, only nearer this time. Fittick stood up and raised his hand. Mungo was striding towards him.

'Blessings, Mungo, and greetings.'

'And to you, too,' said Mungo breathlessly. 'I come to bring some good news, good news of Finn who is recovering and thankful. As are Eilie and Seonaid.'

Nothing of the lepers, Fittick thought. That was still to come.

'And how is Alys?' Fittick was more interested in the child than in his former antagonist. And he wanted to start things on a happier basis, avoiding the gut-wrenching tragedy of the night. Mungo laughed.

'Eating and drinking, laughing, moving around and playing a little. They will not let her do too much, though. Not yet at least.'

'Then that is indeed good news. Thanks be to God.'

And Fittick signed the Cross upon himself. Mungo followed suit.

'And the next thing is, Fittick my friend, of course ...' Mungo's voice trailed off.

Fittick stared down at the garden.

'The lepers?'

'Aye.'

'Was it ... could it be ... strangers to the shore? Maybe from over the hill?'

'You mean – Torry? or even Aberdeen?'

Fittick nodded.

'Why not? It seems to me as possible as ...' He did not finish his sentence. But Mungo picked up his thought.

'One of us, you mean.' This time there was no question in Mungo's voice.

Fittick nodded. Mungo shook his head.

'I left Angus and the elders talking. They are afraid that maybe, perhaps ...' He was unable to finish his thought, but Fittick did it for him.

'One of the youngsters, or maybe more than one,

from Angus's settlement?'

Mungo nodded, head lowered, mouth turned down.

'That's about it.'

'No one has come forward?'

'No!'

'So ... what to do?'

'Eilie and Seonaid are still with Young Nell. Her brother, he ... he ...' Mungo couldn't frame the words.

'Passed on to God?' Fittick asked gently.

'Died!' Mungo roared. 'God help us! He died hideously!'

And he wept.

Died! No gentler word, but died! The words were burned into Fittick's brain, accompanied by vivid memories of burning clothes, blackened stumps of feet and the smouldering hair.

Fittick muttered an apology. Passed on – that was not what had happened. Died hideously, tortured. The horrors of leprosy, then the horrors of a fire, especially one deliberately started, would be forever dug into his consciousness, no matter how he tried to forget, or to cover them over.

Mungo wiped his brow.

'Angus is to hold a meeting with all present, including those of Alasdair's folk. He said to ask if you would be present.'

'That I will.'

'Then, come! Let us go now!' And Mungo whirled back off down the hillside.

Fittick put his tools away and shut his door, with its carving of the risen Christ so gladly carried out in the last few days. He leaned his forehead against Christ's shoulder.

'Lord, help us! Help me!'

Back on shore, trudging along towards Angus's house, Fittick saw what he thought was the entire communities of the shore and hill's edge, gathered in small groups, sitting as family and friends, waiting, silently. The young men were mixed amongst them, with their parents, siblings, and other kinsfolk surrounding them. No time now, no place here, for a band of young men by themselves.

Angus stood as Fittick reached the gathering. He waved Fittick to a cushion of grass near himself, facing the community. Fittick sank down, trying to reduce his presence to be just another member of the community. But Angus was having none of that!

'Priest Fittick,' he boomed. 'I have asked you to be with us and offer a prayer on our behalf to your God. We have already had converse with our own spirits we now want to ensure converse with the Christian God.'

And leave no path unexplored, no stone unturned, no deity ignored, were the superficial thoughts floating into Fittick's mind, as he stood, crucifix raised high. All his thoughts and prayers had prepared him for this, and familiar and much-loved words came easily. What he was not prepared for was the depth of his own emotions, echoing those of the people before him. As he intoned the final pleas, his voice trembled and tears slid down his cheeks.

'We ask your help, O God, we ask blessing on the dead of the family who had suffered so much, and help for the one still alive, still with us.'

There was a resounding Amen, and Fittick sat down again.

Angus stood.

'We want to know. Who did this dreadful thing? We believe the fire was deliberately started – for fear of the lepers, no doubt. We can all share in that. But we have no right to take their lives. So ...' He paused and looked round him. 'Who dared interfere with our human lives? Who dared play god with these people?'

There was a silence, and Fittick as well as Angus, Alasdair and Mungo and the other elders looked intently at the people before them. There might be as many as forty or fifty, thought Fittick, excluding children and elderly who would be unable to climb the hill, or light twigs to burn. And of the remainder, he thought that the women would not do such a thing. So that left – how many? Not that many, and possibly not the older men – but of them, who could say?

There were mutterings, people looked at each other, there was nudging, elbowing, staring. But no one owned up.

Angus shouted again.

'A dastardly deed. But we understand the reason behind it. We are all afeared of this dreadful disease. And we all felt deeply for the suffering of Andrew and Nell, and young Andrew and young Nell.'

The naming of the leprous family unleashed the emotions hidden and held down. Women started to weep, men muttered words like 'dreadful thing', 'terrible cruel', and 'cursed family, why?' But there was no owning up to running up the hillside to the leper home, nor of course to lighting some twigs. Had anyone carried fire with them, from the hearth up the hillside? Or did they rub the twig with small flint pebbles at the fence posts of the dwelling? Whichever way it had been done, it was disturbing.

Angus called out again.

‘I will ask each person – did you know about this? Did you have anything to do with this?’

Fittick stirred. Angus of course would know his people best, but he thought such open questioning might produce a few problems, such as downright lying. Or maybe several mixed answers, confusing to the hearers.

Eilie was the first to move. Angus stared, mouth open in horror, eyes wide.

‘Eilie ... you ... you ...’

‘I will pour some ale for us all, Angus, that will help.’

Despite the circumstances Fittick grinned to himself. Typical Eilie, he thought, as he nodded his thanks for his small cup of ale.

Angus was helpless. The people now were drinking and talking. His questions were unanswered. So far, at any rate.

Angus downed his ale, and found his voice again.

'I ask once more! Anyone with any knowledge of this dreadful deed, please stand, please come forward.'

There was no movement, only the down-turning of heads of men and women, young and old. No one was going to come forward, that was clear. Maybe someone would come forward later, by himself. Or herself. Fittick stood.

'May I speak?'

Angus nodded.

'I am willing to hear if anyone committed this deed and is in misery because of it. The confession will remain secret, of course. But the misery of the one or more who committed this crime may be too much to bear. I am willing to share and pray with that person.'

He sat again. Angus nodded his thanks, and waved to the crowd.

'We are done! You may go to your work.'

'Before we go, Angus, tell us please of Young Nell. Does she yet live?' Eilie had spent the best part of the night caring for the child, and had only reluctantly gone back home in the early hours of the morning.

Angus nodded.

'So far as I know, Eilie, yes, she yet lives.'

So she might be able to point to the criminal, thought Fittick, and saw his thoughts mirrored in Angus's eyes.

CHAPTER TWENTY-ONE

'How are we to care for her?' Eilie wiped her forehead, and the tears from her cheeks. 'She has lost everything, her health, and family and her home. Now what?' Eilie sipped her comforting ale.

'My feeling is that we carry her to the other colony across the hills. I believe they will take her in.' Angus was in charge, as usual, thought Fittick.

'Might it be best if you asked them first, and told them of the fire?' Fittick dared to suggest. 'I do not, of course, know these people as you do, but perhaps they will take pity on her.'

Angus nodded.

'I shall ask Mungo to go and tell them. At a distance, of course! And to request a safe haven for the poor child.'

'She is not yet well enough to be moved, I think. We must wait. But it would be good to know of a home for her.' Eilie continued to sip, as did the others.

'And in the meantime, Eilie, may you and the other women take turns in being with her. So long as ...' and Angus wagged a finger at her, 'you take all precautions, of cover and of washing, and of distance.'

Over the next few days Eilie and her team of carers sat by Young Nell, fed her, tried to wipe the leper spots, and apply healing creams and in particular yarrow butter to the burns. They used long wooden sticks to apply the cream, and burned them after use.

'So the tops which have touched the burns and the leper spots will not harm anything or anyone else.'

Fittick approved of these precautions. It would be so easy to spread the leprosy by leaving these healing sticks in bundles and maybe even considering their re-use. Eilie guessed his thoughts.

'We need to take care, do we not? It is easy to spread a disease.'

'What is in the healing creams?' Fittick was ever curious.

'There are wild carrot tops, and some ramson leaves, in this yarrow butter,' Eilie confided. 'These, along with the yarrow, makes it a superior blend.'

He nodded and hid a grin. Eilie's enthusiasm for her healing creams amused him; her basket was always full of different greeneries, along with the yarrow flowers which luckily abounded over the hillsides.

Not surprisingly Young Nell's recovery was slow. In a week's time she could just manage to sit up, and to feed herself. She allowed the women to stroke yarrow butter on to her wounds, to bathe her with water from the Well, and in so doing, she began to improve physically. But she could scarcely speak for weeping.

'My Da, my Ma, wee Andrew ... how could that be?'

Angus and Fittick left it to Eilie to ask her if she had seen anyone she knew throwing lighted embers into their compound, and she shook her head.

'Naebody, naebody.' And any further questioning or reference to the fire brought on such a fit of weeping and screaming that they deemed it better to leave her in peace.

'So what do we do?' asked Angus helplessly. Fittick glanced at him. Now he was being asked by the headman for advice.

'What do the others think?' He meant of course Alasdair, Eilie, Seonaid and Mungo, those whom he knew best and who seemed to take some leadership in the communities.

Angus sat himself down on the hillside, beside Fittick, and just out of earshot of the dwellings. A few of the men had settled there, quiet, looking out at the sea before the day's work was to begin.

'They are very sure that some of the youngsters took fright at the lepers and decided this way was the best to get rid of them. Maybe make them flee. Not to burn, not themselves, just the houses and fence and the gardens, and the folk themselves just to run away.'

'So it wasn't a deliberate ... execution ... or murder ... or aggression against the family.'

'So the other elders think. More a ploy to get them to leave.'

'Despite some of the yells?'

'Aye, they seemed to be shouting that they wanted the family dead. But most of the community think it was just a bit of ... well, maybe frightening them is the best way of putting it.'

Fittick was unsure. He believed that one or more of the young men were being defended by evading their main purpose, deflecting it into a general, understandable fear. Well, if so, he reflected, that made it easier for him to say a pardon over the whole ghastly offence. He said as much to Angus who brightened up and nodded.

'Aye, a pardon from your God, and maybe from ours, and maybe a ... what do you call it? A penance? Would you have anything in mind?'

Fittick's downcast eyes gleamed. Did he indeed have anything in mind? He looked up.

'Aye, maybe I do. Maybe we can ask Mungo to be part of this talk,' he suggested. 'He is a good man, and he and I have had much conversation on different things.'

Different things? That's one way of putting it, mused Fittick. Different ideas on, say, building a chapel. Maybe that could be helped on by the young men?

'Mungo? Aye, and Finn too. That would include him, make him feel part of things.' He turned and beckoned to Mungo, sitting nearby.

'But would Finn be willing?' Fittick was bemused.

Angus laughed.

'Oh, indeed aye!'

Fittick stared.

'Does this mean ...' His words trailed off. He was unable to articulate his hopes that Finn would drop his enmity. But Mungo had settled beside them, and immediately picked on the unspoken idea.

'Finn is grateful! He may not wish to join you, but he will want to say thank you, for your help. As do his wife and daughter.'

'Is this Eilie's doing? Or Seonaid's? I take it Finn has not sent you here.'

Mungo laughed again.

'Indeed no. It is the work of the women.'

'Then I will accept a gathering in a friendly spirit.' Fittick was clear in his mind. He'd had enough of arguing and fighting. Friendship, hands held out, Anam Cara, as they all said. 'Soul's friendship' - that would be the best thing.

And soul's friendship to the least of people, the leper family. He could not push them out of his mind.

But now to distract him was the thought of a chapel, finding a place for building, laying down the bases, and finding stones and wood for the chapel itself. And, further on, thinking of an altar. He wondered whether he could broach that subject yet.

'First things first,' he said aloud. Washed up on the shores of Aberdeen, near the village of Torry, living at the Bay of Nigg – and all in the space of a few weeks. He reminded himself of his Bishop's words. *Take it slowly, Fittick. Do not rush at things*. 'I will be very keen to accept an invitation to such a gathering. When is it to be?'

'It needs to be soon, I believe,' said Mungo. 'While what happened is still fresh in the mind.'

Angus nodded.

'This evening. Unless something happens to stop it.'

'Good,' said Mungo, 'but I must go and fish now. I shall come back in time.' He raised a hand and started towards the shore.

'Stop!' yelled Fittick after him. 'You have not even had a warm drink in my company this morning.'

Mungo waved back.

'I'm off to the boats, man, fishing inshore is good today. I'll save something for you.' And he ran down the short hillside through the tall sedges to the shore

CHAPTER TWENTY-TWO

Fittick peered after him. There were several boats bobbing in the water and Mungo made for the first one, where a crew of two other men were waiting. He jumped on board, and the two crewmen pushed the boat out into the waters, and followed him on board.

'In, out! In, out!'

Fittick could just hear the voices as they took the oars up and rowed the boat out to the fishing grounds.

'Hope they get a good catch,' he thought. 'I could be doing with some fresh fish.'

On board, Mungo was steering carefully, with an eye on the birdlife. Flocks on the sea's surface were always a sure sign of fish gathering. But today he had other thoughts in his mind, too.

Seonaid. Seonaid and himself.

Until Fittick had appeared, he had had a mind to approach Seonaid, as more than a friend. He had been slow to approach, he admitted, but, and again he thought, marriage is a big thing, and I wanted to move around, to travel, to try different things. Was I ready to take a wife? Am I ready now?

But now things had changed. Seonaid had shown a fondness for Fittick. Would that continue? He was aware that Fittick could, if he wished, take a wife. Celibacy was not an absolute law. But in one of their friendly debates Fittick had intimated that he had taken a vow of celibacy and would not break it. He had said that a wife and family would distract him from his main purpose, that of preaching the gospel, and of following Christ.

But men have been known to change their minds before. Might Fittick take back his vow? Mungo thought that Fittick had shown some warmth to Seonaid, but was it enough to make him change from that vow of celibacy? He shrugged. Too difficult for me to think out now, he decided. Fishing, that's the thing, that's where I need to concentrate.

Fittick was also struggling with deep thoughts. Seonaid! She had reappeared in his thoughts, in connection with Mungo's appearance. They were coupled together in Fittick's mind. And he began to rethink his feelings. Yes, it could be, but no it could not be. What was most important? I must think this out again! And he decided to take a long walk, to meditate, to pray and to try to come to some permanent solution.

He strode off along the hillside, turned left at a seeming path and began again the climb to the burned-out leper dwellings. The path was stony and narrow, the grass was thick, and the distant mooing of the cows made it likely to be good stuff for eating. Blue skies and a bright sun warmed his body, his feet made their way carefully over the clumps of long-stemmed slightly hairy grass, interspersed with yarrow and plantain, he noticed. There was a soft buttercup yellow flower, but not a buttercup. And a taller-growing, yellow-flowered plant, with sharper leaves. And a scattering of starry white flowers dotted amongst the grassy mounds. Fittick was ignorant of most plants, and was not himself a practical hands-on healer, but he wondered whether these plants were of use in the medicines which Eilie, for one, was forever concocting.

He reached the top of the hill. As usual, he gazed at the big bay below him, and beyond the bay were some small structures, made of he knew not what. They looked like stone buildings, sturdy and strong.

Further round the bay, down to his left, were more huts along busy paths. He could just see people moving along, in and out of the houses, children trotting beside the adults.

And in the bay itself was a small fleet of boats, pulled up on to the shore. Men were working on these boats, Fittick could see. They were heaving nets on board, they were fitting the oars into the rowlocks, they were fitting cross-bars neatly for the rowers to sit on. A busy place, he reflected, men and women about their business. He had seen some of this before but not in such numbers. The women had baskets on their backs and they were hurrying from a gathering of people just beyond the shore. Looks like a market, thought Fittick, impressed by this spectacle of industry. Fish landed, fish to sell, women taking the fish to sell, maybe taking the fish to gut and smoke as Mungo had told him. He thought he would like to know more of this, the curing of the fish, the cooking and flavouring of it.

Sighing, he turned away, back towards the leper dwelling. There was so much to do, so much to know, and so much to think about. The fishwives had set him thinking again about Seonaid, and how attractive would be a small house, with her care and cooking, and her love for him. And he finally admitted to himself, he loved her as man to woman.

He fingered his crucifix again. Would he have taken such vows had he known Seonaid earlier?

Mungo, carefully steering his currach, was thinking the same thoughts. He had had adventure, he had had travel, he had explored and met people, tried the monastic life, decided to return home to sail and fish. He loved company but he also craved solitude, the peace and quiet of meditation, of considering the world around him, the hours of living, moment by moment, learning and doing. And there was peace of mind in not having to consider another person, in not talking, listening, or just being with someone. What would be the advantage of marriage? Maybe companionship in the lonely times. Because there were lonely times in the alone-ness of solitude, as he was sure Fittick knew too. And not just the companionship, he thought, but the bedding of such a woman, the union of their two bodies. That might bring children of such a union. At that thought Mungo chuckled to himself. A son like himself? Not so! He remembered his childhood as a busy, exploring, investigating, and disobedient period of life, working when he had to, but rushing round the shores looking at plants, at stones, watching buildings being erected, watching boats being built. And scarcely ever at home. His mother had always worried about him.

‘Hoi! Hoi!’ one of the crewmen yelled at him. He

blinked and rubbed his eyes. The men had stopped rowing, and were pulling in the dragnet at the stern of the boat.

'We need to empty this net, Mungo,' said one of the crew. 'Just you take a look at this.' And he heaved the net above the sea level. It was full of wriggling fish, flumping and thumping against each other in their attempts to escape.

'Not a bad catch,' added the other crewman. 'We'll empty it, and send it down again.'

Mungo was delighted. He had steered towards this patch in the sea, far from shore, because he had seen a flock of seabirds soaring and diving. Clearly a sign of fish, he had thought then, and he was right. There was a good catch in that area, and maybe more to come.

The wriggling fish were emptied into boxes on the deck, and the dragnet was sent off again hopefully to get more. No more time for meditation, Mungo thought, back to work, search the waters, watch the birds, look for any signs of shoals. And get on with the job.

CHAPTER TWENTY-THREE

Seonaid sat by the hearth stirring the stew pot. It smelt delicious and she wanted to make sure the meat didn't stick to the base and burn. She wanted, if she were completely truthful, to make sure Fittick knew what a delicious meal she made and what care she took to cook it. How he was to know this she wasn't sure, but at the back of her mind the thought of pleasing him, getting him to admire her handiwork and to see her in a pleasing light, was of huge importance.

A noise seized her attention. She stared at Finn, rising from the bed space where he and Eilie slept. He looked gaunt, his bed clothes wrinkled down to his bare feet, his beard straying and uncombed, unusually for him. His hair, too, lay unkempt about his shoulders, and in wild locks above his brow and over his ears.

'My father! My father!' gasped Seonaid. 'Are you well enough to be on your feet?'

'Aye, lass, aye. I feel better, much better, and …' He

held up his hands. 'Don't tell me. I know! It is thanks to yon Christian man, him that I didna like, him that I sent about his business and him that I raised my fist tae.'

'He wouldn't mind. He wouldn't. He's a nice man, a decent man. He'd understand,' Seonaid murmured passionately.

'I make no doubt.' Finn wrinkled his brows thoughtfully. 'No, I make no doubt about that. But it must be put right from my side. Else I will not feel right. I need to make my thanks.'

He sat down by the hearth and held out his hand for a bowl of stew.

'And a bannock, please, my daughter. Just a small one.'

Seonaid tended to his needs as best she could. Her concern was that he should not eat and drink too much so soon after the fever had left him. He needed to rest and recover. But she well knew that if she told him that, he would become upset and angry with her. She wished Eilie were back from her plant gathering and her medicine making.

Finn supped slowly, chewed his bannock, and slowly wiped the crumbs off his matted beard and from his bed attire. He was obviously thinking hard, with his brow furrowed and his eyes narrowed.

‘Mind you!’ he rapped out at last. ‘Mind this! I will make up with the man, I will tell him that I can now thole his God. But I do not want you going too close to him and his God, by yourself or with your friends.’

She was annoyed, and forgot her resolve of gentle agreement and of not opposing him.

‘You cannot forbid me, father, I am of age.’

Some of her friends would meekly agree with Finn, with his father’s authority. Seonaid had no mind to do so. Whether Finn approved or not, her heart belonged with Fittick, she was sure.

Fittick thumped his stick on the ground, but weakly.

‘You are my daughter. You will marry when I consider the man fit for you. I will choose your husband.’

Her eyes sparked fury. She opened her mouth to protest, but was stopped by something in his slumped posture, his unusual slovenly attitude and grubby clothes. This man was not capable of thinking clearly, and would be hurt and angry if she opposed and fought him and his ideas. He might even become more sick.

And she was also a practical young woman.

Pondering over Fittick's attitudes, his single-minded focus in this settlement, his ambitions to take the Gospels further, she wondered how it would be if Fittick insisted on maintaining his calling. She sighed. Life was not simple. All it should contain was family and food, but to achieve those there was much work, and a great deal of thought. She got up to collect some more firewood to feed the hearth fire and continue the cooking. Food for the belly, that was important. Food for the soul – well, who knew what that might be. Would it also bring comfort for the body? Whatever that comfort might mean.

Finn stirred on his cushion. He was fond of his daughter, the only child left to him, to nurture him in his old age, he thought. As a practical man, he thought of his own wellbeing, and his growing older in the settlement, with wife and daughter and maybe grandchildren to run and do his bidding. And he himself at the head and centre. That dream pleased him. But how to make it happen? Finn sighed. Had it not been for that vicious storm which took his elder daughter and her husband from him, there would have been more in his family circle.

The atmosphere was heavy with thoughts. Little Alys stirred under her bedclothes and looked at her grandfather, then at her aunt. But unusually neither of them was watching her.

Seonaid was thinking of the storm that took her sister's life. How she had envied her sister her happiness, her marriage with someone she loved, her child and the prospect of more to come. That last fateful voyage was vivid in Seonaid's mind. She remembered waving to her sister as she boarded the boat with her husband, both of them laughing and joyful at the thought of a sail by themselves, he would steer, she would row. Then she would steer and he would row. They would have fun. Seonaid could see them now, waving, faces alight with joy.

Wasn't that what she wanted too?

Yet, if she continued to pursue Fittick, then she might, almost certainly would, have to leave the settlement and go with him to another home, to a different people. She was sure he would not wish to remain in the small settlements here but would want to try for another, larger place. And who would then care for Alys, as Eilie became older? Who would help Eilie with Finn? Who would care for their small family?

A cooling of the hearth pulled her attention back to the job in hand. Feed the fire, feed the flame – the real flame, the hearth fire, not the wisps of the imagined future. Seonaid pushed some more sticks into the centre of the hearth. The flames burned up again, and the food continued to sizzle.

A thudding of boots in the doorway drew the attention of both Finn and Seonaid from their own musings. Eilie came in carrying an armful of bags with stems poking out of the tops, and by the bulging look of them, thought Seonaid, she had had a good harvest. Seonaid could identify fennel, plantain and comfrey, a useful all-purpose healing plant, and the flowers were pretty. She stood up.

'Come, mother Eilie, come in and warm yourself. You have been busy, have you not?'

Alys tottered to be with them, to bury her nose in the scents, and finger the flowerheads. Eilie was triumphant as she spread her bagfuls of healing plants by the hearth.

'Yes, I shall be busier still when I have treated these and created some healing from them. And,' she paused, looking carefully at Finn. 'I am minded to ask yon priest about any medicines he knows of.'

Finn gripped his lips together, and Seonaid could see that her father was still reluctant to think well of Fittick, though he knew that by right, he needed to make some sort of reparation to Fittick and to thank him for his help. Finn swirled his bedclothes around him.

'You may speak with him, wife! You may! And I shall also hold some converse with him.'

With a flourish of his blanket, he strode away to dress. Seonaid lowered her head and tried not to giggle too loudly. Eilie was chuckling too.

'See how we move on,' she laughed, as she picked up her small mortar and pestle ready to start grinding the plant stems.

'Maybe you should dry them first,' suggested Seonaid.

'Some I will dry, some I will pound to dry later,' her mother answered placidly, moving the pestle club round the bowl filled with comfrey.

Finn came striding over, clad in tunic and breeches.

'My boots! I wish for my boots!'

Seonaid rushed over to the corner where his boots were always kept.

'Here, Father. Let me help you.'

Finn sat and stretched out one foot for Seonaid to fit on his strong leather boot. First one, then the other fitted on his thick hose, and he pulled them up to encase his thin calves comfortably.

'You must be going far, Father. Are you well enough now?' Seonaid, ever practical, stood holding his cloak.

‘I do but go to visit our priestly friend, on the hillside.’ Fittick swung his cloak round his shoulders. ‘I may be some time.’

‘Father, are you fit enough?’

‘Finn, my man, let me come with you. You may be in need of help. Your recovery is not yet complete.’ Eilie picked up her own cloak.

‘Not so. I go by myself.’ And he swung through the door, walking firmly and with purpose.

Seonaid and Eilie glanced at each other. There was no stopping Finn if he had made up his mind to do something.

Alys set up a wail, demanding attention, and Finn’s journey was forgotten in the need and delight in tending the convalescent child.

CHAPTER TWENTY-FOUR

On the hillside, Fittick sought to calm his restlessness. He longed for the same spiritual experience which he'd had there before. But today none was forthcoming. He was left with his own thoughts.

He watched as the slow procession of locals picked up young Nell from the leper dwelling in her litter, and made its way across the hill towards the second leper settlement, near Torry. They had agreed willingly to take in Young Nell and she would be cared for, and loved, he thought, until ... well, until she too died.

He raised his hand in blessing.

'God go with you,' he shouted.

Turning his back on the wider view from the hilltop, Fittick turned to scramble back down to his hermit dwelling. He was tired. The walks along the shore and up the hill were too much, he thought. But that view, that place – and just beyond was where Machar had been. One hundred years ago, this man had worked so nearby, this beloved, this missionary, this explorer, this companion – Fittick paused in wonder – of Columba, the great Irish missionary of Christ. Fittick had known about Columba since his early years. And he had heard of Machar, too, as one of his companions on the journey from Ireland, in his preaching on the Isle of Mull, in his curing of the lepers there. And he knew of Columba's order to Machar to establish a church where the river formed the crook of a bishop's crozier. Machar had found the place on the river Don, up to the north, and had built. Fittick decided that was a journey he had to make.

But in the meantime, back to the fisherfolk of the Bay. As he looked down on his hermitage, he saw a figure standing by the door, hand upraised as if to knock or push the door open. Fittick wondered. It was definitely one of the elders. He picked up speed to reach his small dwelling as fast as possible.

He reached his doorway, silent-footed on the quiet hillside. Finn turned.

'I have come to say thank you, sir priest.' His words were formal and his voice sounded harsh. Was he really thankful, Fittick wondered, or angry that his own kind had not cured him but the Christian God had done so?

'Welcome, Finn. And no need of thanks. We have all thanked our God and His Son, Christ Jesus.' Fittick opened the door of his dwelling and ushered Finn into the small room. Finn sank down on a cushioned stone beside the fire's ashes. Fittick hurried to rekindle the fire, rubbing sticks roughly between his hands and pushing the lighted twigs into the hearth. It was a constant delight to see the fire begin its flames, soft and small at first, then growing upwards, licking through the wood of the hearth.

'This is like our God, Finn,' said Fittick softly. 'He works small, and slow, and gradually upwards and inwards, to tell people of His goodness and love, until it is shared amongst all, and we all catch the flame.'

Finn gritted his teeth.

'Our Cailleach, our Aengus, our gods work well.'

'Indeed they do, of that I make no doubt.' Fittick was quick to agree. 'But do they reach out to all, with all-knowingness and love? Or do they keep to their own activities?'

'We can pray to each god as we need,' Finn growled. 'We need no others.'

'Should some of our family wish to know and accept the all-knowing, all-loving God, what harm is there in extending friendship to Him and His Son?' Fittick was persuasive. He handed Finn a cup of ale.

'Friendship? Friendship, you say? Can gods be friendly amongst each other?'

'Indeed, and why not? They are gods, they look after us, they hear us. Why not hear each other too?'

'You speak words that bring deep thought, sir priest.'

'Fittick, sir.'

'Fittick, then, thank you.' Finn almost smiled. 'I will keep thinking of what you say, but for myself, I want none of it.'

'But you will not prevent others learning?'

Finn shook his head.

'No, not prevent learning.' Now his tone was hesitant. 'But, sir … Fittick …'

Fittick grinned behind his hand. Was this use of his name a move towards some lightening of his acceptance of the Christian God? He hoped so, but it amused him.

'Please go on, sir.' Fittick's tone was courteous towards the older man.

'I want nothing like it in our family!'

'Eilie, your wife, and …' Fittick hesitated, 'your daughter too have an interest.'

Finn nodded.

'Eilie, yes, and ah yes, it is my daughter of whom I wish to speak.'

Fittick waited, nervously.

'I wish for her to marry amongst her own kind! I have noticed she has a tenderness towards you, but I do not wish this to go any further.' He brought his fist down with a thump on the hearthstone. The flames jumped a little, the sticks twisted and crackled.

Fittick felt chilled despite the heat. This was frankness indeed. Frank and open about the gods and their part, and even more so about Seonaid. As indeed he had a right to be. Fittick's mind was clear on the father's duty - a duty to care for and direct his daughter. He bit his lip. Her fondness for him must have been noticed, and no doubt his response to her. Now there were two reasons to pull back from loving her. One of course was his wish to serve Christ wherever he might be needed, just like both Machar and Columba. The second reason he had not foreseen. The care of a father for his daughter, and his wish for her to remain amongst the familiar people of their countryside.

It was a wish to be respected. And he would respect it.

He bowed.

'It shall be as you wish, sir.'

'Thank you.' Finn got slowly to his feet. 'And in return, sir priest, er … Fittick, I shall rouse my followers to parley with you in friendship. And more, I believe – if I have heard rightly – that you wish for a chapel to your God. My followers and I shall assist in building a chapel … if that is your wish.'

Fittick stared in astonishment. Finn smiled and pulled at his beard.

'Is it not so with the Christians? I have heard, from those who have travelled, and from visits in Aberdeen, that chapels are places of worship for Christians.'

'Indeed, it is so,' stammered Fittick, 'but I had not thought …' His voice trailed away. 'Your generosity of spirit, Finn, it is, well, I mean ...' he stuttered again, completely taken aback.

Finn smiled again and raised his hand.

'Farewell for the moment, to one whom I wish to call my friend.'

And he turned and left Fittick's dwelling.

Fittick was open-mouthed, and still stood there amazed as Mungo arrived.

CHAPTER TWENTY-FIVE

Mungo looked nervous, biting his lip, gulping. And also slightly stunned, as if something had happened to surprise him greatly.

Fittick felt much the same.

‘Mungo, my friend,’ he began.

Mungo held up his hand.

‘Wait. You might not call me friend when you hear what I have to say.’

Fittick groaned.

‘Not you, too. I have had some converse with Finn and I am somewhat taken aback. He offered me …’

‘Wait!’ begged Mungo. ‘Please wait! One whom I hoped to call friend forever, this might not happen.’

Fittick gestured to the glowing hearth.

‘Sit, Mungo, sit. And we will have some conversation.’

Mungo slammed himself down on a cushioned seat.

'I want to say,' he began.

'Wait.' Fittick stopped him. 'I need some heartening ale after my talk with Finn, positive though it was. Let me bring you some too.' Fittick went to the hearth and ladled some warm ale into two cups.

'Here, sip, and warm your heart.'

Mungo took the tankard doubtfully.

'It may need more than this for both of us.'

Fittick took his place beside his friend. He poked the hearth and added some twigs to make it glow brighter.

'Now tell me,' he ordered.

Mungo gulped down a mouthful.

'This morning, I went fishing. I went in my currach and we brought back a goodly load of white fish. The men were pleased, needless to say, as was I.' He stopped and supped again. Fittick sighed inwardly. Was this to be a fishing story gone wrong? Or was it about the crew? Or what? He could only wait.

'It was a calm day. The steering was good. The sight of the sea, the distance from the land, the hillscape clean and clear against the light. I felt good. I felt at home. I felt a closeness. I felt I belonged.'

'And then?'

'In belonging, and maybe being so familiar here I felt …' Mungo stammered. He seemed unsure how to describe his feelings.

'Go on. Say it as it comes, we can make sense of it later.'

'I felt I wanted to put down roots. To make a real home of it. Here. At the Bay. Maybe in Torry itself.'

'How did you see this happening?'

Mungo bit his lips and pulled his sleeve across his eyes.

'Fittick, I have seen, I have observed … what I have noticed is …' There was a silence. Then Mungo went on. 'I have noticed that perhaps you and … Seonaid might have some warmth between you.'

There! It was out! It was spoken. It could not be taken back.

Fittick took a deep breath. How was he to answer this? It was true. There was warmth, there had perhaps been a move towards closeness. But as well as his own vows, there was also what Finn had said to him earlier in the day.

‘And so?’

‘And so, I wondered about you. Because,’ Mungo was clearly nervous. ‘Because I have my own feelings about her, and perhaps were it not for you, she might return my warmth.’

‘You think Seonaid would prefer me to you?’ Fittick chuckled, trying to lighten the darkness between them.

‘Yes. Yes, I do.’

Would he confess to his own feelings, Fittick wondered, or just remind Mungo of his priestly vow of celibacy? But he must repeat what Finn had said. Maybe that was enough? Carefully he set down his empty cup.

‘Let me tell you, Mungo, that Finn thought like you, and has warned me that he wishes Seonaid to become handfasted to a man likely to remain in the community. To one whom he knows, and one who would not take her away.’

‘But Seonaid has a mind of her own,’ Mungo began.

‘True! And that is something I have witnessed. Her strength and her thoughtfulness are part of her … attraction.’

Eagerly Mungo agreed.

‘She’s kind and good to everyone.’

‘But,’ Fittick continued, ‘I must also confess that my own feelings had become involved. I knew my wish to be on my own early in my priesthood. And no, my early choices are not binding. If I chose to marry, it would be possible, and I could still continue my priesthood.’

‘And is that … is that what you wish to do?’

‘I have given it much thought since I realised my own feelings and the possibility that Seonaid might feel warmth towards me.’ Fittick poked the hearth again, hiding his expressions of doubt. ‘As I have taken my walks over the hills, I have thought much. And as I have walked by the shores, listening to the seas, I have thought much. But what persuaded me to pursue my vow of celibacy was my visit to the lepers. No,’ he held up a hand. ‘I did not go near them. It was nothing like that – I am safe. But their suffering and their joy in talking with an outsider was heart-warming. And when I told them of Christ and His own suffering, what they spoke of was love towards this Man.’

‘How so?’ Mungo was bewildered.

‘That someone would willingly suffer for such as we all are, including our lepers, that God so loved the world that He gave His Son – they took that as a sign of caring.'

'And lepers have little enough of caring in their lives,' Mungo remarked.

'Just so. And I have promised to return to those lepers further along the hillside, and talk more. And when we build our chapel, to make it certain that in some way they can come to chapel even to stand outside in a particular place, where they are not complete outcasts. There is a link, to us, and to God. He will not turn from them.'

'I understand so far, but what has this to do with my own life?'

'It means, for me,' said Fittick slowly, drawing a pattern on the hearth ashes, 'that I maintain my priestly calling as an unmarried man. That I devote myself to God and Christ through ministering to his people on earth. That my whole being is for Christ alone. No woman, no family will enter my life and take my attention away.'

There was a profound silence. Mungo sat, his hopes raised again, and his admiration for his friend unbounded. He felt, he thought, exalted. Tears gathered and slid down his cheeks.

Fittick sat, head bowed, hand on his crucifix. Presently he looked up and smiled.

‘Go to her, Mungo, my friend, always to be my friend. Ask for her in marriage, ask to be handfasted. And say you both have my blessing.’

CHAPTER TWENTY-SIX

But the business with the leper house fire was not yet finished. Angus called a meeting of all people on the hillside, and included those living in Torry as well.

When everyone was assembled – and it made a goodly crowd, thought Fittick – Angus stood up.

'I have called us together, good people, to say that no one has admitted to setting fire to the leper house. But,' and he paused dramatically, 'we believe it to have been done to force the lepers to leave and *not* to kill them.'

There was a loud murmur of agreement as neighbours turned to neighbours and nodded, and young men looked sideways at each other and grinned slyly. Women smiled.

'So though we do not approve of the enforcement, we will not pursue the people who created the fire. We will deprecate it, and we will suggest that all of us had a hand in it, since we have not cared enough for the lepers. We needed to do better. We need to do better.'

He turned to Fittick.

'Sir priest, the words are with you.'

Fittick stood up, cloak swirling about his ankles. He raised his crucifix and stood waiting until all had fixed their eyes on it and on him.

'What was done was a sin!' he shouted. 'But Angus and the elders are in the right of it. Murder was not the deliberate intention. Fear of contagion, wanting to move the lepers away from the settlements, was the sin. And fear can lead to bad consequences.'

He paused. There were mutterings, but most of the crowd was still and quiet, waiting for more.

'While I cannot forgive sinners individually on behalf of the risen Christ, I can forgive them whose elders have testified on their behalf. Angus, Finn, Alasdair and the senior men have expressed sorrow and will to do better in the future, and to adopt the idea of a caring God who will meet with your own gods. We will become one community, with our gods and the Christian God caring for us. We will learn care and love from the Christian God and His Son, the Risen Christ. That is what He teaches. Love and care for all. Forgiveness of sins – for as He said of those who mocked him, "they know not what they do". Our people acted in ignorance and fear. Therefore they can be forgiven. And in the Name of the Father, the Son and the Holy Spirit, I can and do forgive them.'

He raised his crucifix on high and shouted ‘Amen!’

And all – or almost all – shouted Amen in chorus with him.

Angus was again on his feet.

‘Fittick has suggested that for full forgiveness there be a penance. And the penance your elders and Alasdair, Finn and I have agreed to is the building of a chapel to the Christian God.’

Fittick glanced round. Finn was beaming at his inclusion amongst the headmen. Alasdair was nodding, and Angus watching all the fishermen carefully.

There was some discussion amongst the families. Some men were nodding, some shaking their heads. Some were standing, saying Not so. Others agreed. It took some time for the meeting to come to any sort of conclusion, and not until some of the young men had been jostled into the centre, and had been shaken somewhat, was any conclusion reached.

But as the sun was darkening, as the day was drawing to its close, the words which Fittick had hoped to hear came forth.

‘We will do it! We will begin tomorrow!’

CHAPTER TWENTY-SEVEN

There was much to be done before the chapel could actually be built. A site must be chosen, amenable to all, foundations laid, sufficient building material to be selected, and a design to be thought of. The builders had not seen many chapels. Fittick was busy, as was Mungo.

Halfway up the hillside was the selected site. Building materials of wood and stone were all round. The locals who had use of it agreed to the new use of the land.

And most important, the best builders from both shoreside communities offered their services.

It was done, and done quickly. Foundations were laid one fine day when it was too sunny and warm for fishing. Then at intervals different builders came and laid stones alongside each other to shape the walls. Fittick looked on and marvelled. It was a small chapel, but then, these were small communities and would crowd in comfortably.

The earth was to be kept bare, partially, said Fittick,

to help move the building on quickly and to finish the job, and partly also to remind everyone whence they came and to what they would return.

Men came from Torry, and from further inland, from Aulton, Machar's settlement. One of these latter beckoned to Fittick as he was watching the builders, and led him aside into his hut.

'I bring you an offering, sir priest.'

Fittick smiled. He was still in a state of astoundment at the building of the chapel. Fittick's church, Fittick's chapel, as the fisherfolk were calling it. An offering from someone in Aberdeen was but grist to the mill.

'Thank you, kind sir. I do appreciate your kindness, and perhaps the elders might know of this as well?'

The man from Aulton nodded.

'Please do call them hither.'

Fittick went back to the hillside and beckoned Finn and Angus to tell them of his visitor. He invited Mungo as well. While he now had a better command of the local dialect, he felt it useful to have an interpreter, one who could make clear what was happening. And he had to ensure his friendship with Mungo – though he secretly envied Mungo his attachment to Seonaid, he had made his decision. He was happy for them both, and intended to show it by offering a blessing on them as they became handfasted.

The three men returned with Fittick to the hut where the man from Aulton sat placidly. He waved aside all offers of food and drink and said,

'I come only to offer a gift. You may wish to discuss this amongst yourselves and come to me to tell me of your decision. Or I can wait a little today while you talk.'

Impatiently Fittick waited to hear of the offering.

'It is that our community of Christians in Aberdeen, those of us who follow the tradition of Machar, wish to offer you an altar. It is of wood, carved with the image of Christ on the Cross, and can be transported here in a day.'

Overwhelmed, Fittick could only stammer his delight. Angus held up a hand.

'Wait, Fittick, wait. Should our altar be of wood? Or of stone?'

The visitor smiled, and nodded.

'That is indeed subject for discussion. It might help you to know that this altar was blessed by the holy Machar himself.'

‘Why do you kindly offer us this gift?’ Finn wanted to know.

‘We do so to welcome another gathering of Christians to our community. And because we ourselves are possessed of another such, also blessed by Machar and by Colman also. We would wish to share.’

Fittick could only bow his head and wait for the others to speak. For himself he was keen to accept this munificence, but the elders had caused the chapel to be built, therefore the elders should be part of the gift’s acceptance. As he had no doubt it would be accepted.

And he was right. Angus smiled broadly and reached out to shake the hand of the visitor. Finn nodded.

‘Indeed, sir, we welcome your gift and thank you and your community. An altar, blessed by Machar, would indeed be of first importance in our small chapel.’

Fittick smiled inwardly at the use of the word ‘our’. The chapel had been the means of uniting factions amongst the settlements and indeed ensuring good friendship between those on the shore-side.

‘What think you, Fittick, our priest?’ Angus turned to him. Fittick stood and bowed to his visitor. ‘With our elders’ permission, indeed I am more than grateful, and will thank Christ for your offer and with your permission, will pray for you.'

The visitor smiled and stood.

'Then I shall see that it is carried over to you tomorrow.'

With that he left, and the men remained, open-mouthed, until Finn, ever practical, asked,

'At which end of the chapel, Fittick?'

'On the east side, Finn.'

'Then let us go and prepare a place.'

CHAPTER TWENTY-EIGHT

And so it was done.

The altar was in place, and the walls grew up round it.

And as windows were placed in the walls, one window in particular was built in a special way.

Fittick explained his reasons in the Stone Circle, where he was now a regular and welcome visitor to any community discussions.

'You all know that on the further hillside there, there is a small community suffering from the fell skin disease of leprosy, contagious and frightening. God knew of lepers, Christ healed lepers when He could. Therefore it ill becomes us to shun them.'

'But …' There were many protests around the Circle. 'This is a dread disease. We could catch it from these people. They must not come to our chapel. You must not see them.'

'If we made special arrangements,' began Fittick, but

again was shouted down. Patiently he waited, watching the faces for sympathisers as well as keeping an eye on the opposing people.

Mungo waved a hand in the air. He wanted to say something. Angus nodded to him.

'Speak, Mungo.'

'Might we know what arrangements you have in mind, Fittick?'

'That no way do the lepers come into the chapel, but only to a special place, marked off for them, in the church yard, and they come to a special window, which will show them only the altar and the offering of Christ on the Cross. The congregation will not even see them, nor they the congregation.'

And so it was done. The window, known as 'the leper's squint', was installed on the east side of the chapel, near the altar, facing only to the altar. The lepers were to walk in a straight line, between fencing, to the window, and after the service, return again to their home on the further hillside.

Came the day the chapel was finished – and major celebrations were in order. Mungo approached Fittick hesitantly.

'My friend, if I may still call you so, can I crave a boon?'

Fittick knew what was coming, and braced himself.

'It is only that Seonaid and I became handfasted, as you know, some weeks ago. And we thought perhaps we might have a Christian wedding in the chapel.'

Fittick laid his hand on Mungo's shoulder.

'My friend, you and Seonaid are well-suited, as I said at the time of handfasting. A wedding there shall be indeed! Let us begin our chapel celebrations with the wedding of Mungo and Seonaid.'

Mungo beamed. He had not wanted to lose friendship with Fittick, whom he liked and admired. But he had not been sure of Fittick's feelings since his own handfasting with Seonaid. Now, it seemed, all was well.

And indeed, the chapel was blessed, and the wedding was held, at the altar of Machar, and with the grace of the congregation as benefactors to the new couple in their midst.

At the end of the day, when Mungo and Seonaid had gone to their own new home, Angus and Finn visited Fittick. The friendship amongst the three men had grown with the construction of the chapel, and Fittick no longer felt that Finn was against the Christians. Fittick relaxed in their company, could discuss private anxieties and other matters with them, could talk freely, as had been his wont with his Bishop in France.

He offered them warm ale. Angus and Finn produced the usual gift of bannocks from their wives.

'What now, my friend?' asked Angus. 'Will you be content to live among us and minister to us?'

Fittick had been wondering the same thing himself. Could he stay in one place? Would it be the Bishop's wish?

'For myself, Angus, yes, I would be content. Perhaps a bit of roaming, maybe to Colman's monastery and especially to Machar's people. But yes, remaining is my wish.'

Angus smiled and Finn raised his cup.

'Then you are truly one of us.'

SOURCES

Aberdeen Maritime Museum:

https://www.aberdeencity.gov.uk/AAGM/plan-your-visit/aberdeen-maritime-museum

https://doriccolumns.wordpress.com/water-supply/ancient-wells/st-fitticks-well/

Gazetteer for Scotland ©2022 The Editors of The Gazetteer for Scotland
Supported by: School of GeoSciences, University of Edinburgh and The Royal Scottish Geographical Society

Aberdeenshire Council History:

https://online.aberdeenshire.gov.uk/smrpub/master/detail.aspx?refno=NJ90SE0001

Thomas White Ogilvie, *The Book of St Fittick*

https://electricscotland.com/books/saint_fittick.htm
#

The Rotary Club of St Fittick

https://www.rotary-ribi.org/clubs/homepage.php?ClubID=2

Saintsplaces.gla.ac.uk

https://www.undiscoveredscotland.co.uk/aberdeen/stfitticks/index.html

Archaeologist Ali Cameron describes the project at St Fittick's Church, at Nigg to record the standing buildings and gravestones and an excavation at the adjacent manse.

https://www.youtube.com/watch?v=zSbcly0_fyc&t=10s

About the Author:

Beatrice Hale is Aberdeen born and bred, but now lives in New Zealand where she draws on the vibrant tales from her family history for her books for adults and children.

Also by Beatrice Hale:

Ice Escape

MAYDAY, MAYDAY, MAYDAY. This is flight Foxtrot, Alpha, 092 calling Angmassalik …

1932

John wants to be part of the first family to fly around the world. Colin wants to stay at home, not sail out on a fishing trawler into the Arctic Ocean where his father drowned.

But one little accident leads to disaster, and that means the boys have to overcome their fears for an adventure from home, in one of the coldest, harshest places on earth.

The Resolute Heart

A determined woman …

When Napoleon is threatening the shores of Britain, Nelson's navy needs all the men it can get – and they're not all volunteers.

Mary's husband is snatched from the shores of Fife to serve in the biggest naval battle of the age. But Mary's no sit-at-home wife: she's going after him.

On the way she'll make enemies and friends – sometimes it's hard to tell which is which. Not everyone wants Nelson to win.

Will she find Harry? And if she does, can she rescue him – from the navy and from the country's worst enemies?

Printed in Great Britain
by Amazon

86624617R00171